DOGGED PURSUIT

"I propose to give them a portion of your clothing to familiarize them with your scent," said Bognor's tormentor. "Then you may take a ten-minute start to swim across the lake from the island. Normally this exercise would destroy your trail, but I think my breeding has given these animals a highly developed nose to get over that. In any case they have all the time in the world to find you, though the sooner they do the happier we shall all be."

Bognor sensed the malevolent smile though he could not see it . . .

Let Sleeping Dogs Die

Tim Heald

BALLANTINE BOOKS • NEW YORK

FOR
ALEXANDER

Prologue

It was scarcely dawn as Champion Whately Wonderful of Three Corners, better known to his friends as Fred, pushed an anticipatory muzzle round the front door of his kennel. Pausing outside, he peered about him, sniffing the cool Home Counties air. It was too early yet for his owner, Mrs Ailsa Potts, also of Three Corners of Surblington, Bucks, to be about. Too early, too, for the kennelmaids. Champion Whately Wonderful stretched his hind legs and sniffed at the high barbed wire. There had been a noise of some sort and there was a smell which was appetizing. He loped to the wire netting and sprang up on his hind legs, leaning his front paws in front of him for support. Standard poodles didn't come finer than Whately Wonderful with his shining black coat cut in the regulation French style, his high domed head and clear intelligent eyes. Success in next week's Windsor show would make him one of the half-dozen top dogs in Britain and a leading contender for next winter's Cruft's.

The dog got down from the netting and started to pace round the perimeter of the run. Somewhere he could smell meat, and he rolled the skin back off his teeth and gave a low whine as he set about his search. It was scarcely light yet and none of the dogs in the adjacent kennels had stirred. In itself that was not surprising. Champion Whately Wonderful was a notoriously light sleeper. He continued pacing along the wire until he turned the second corner, the one nearest the entrance to the kennels, and froze. There, on the grass about two feet inside his territory, was a large slab of raw sirloin steak. For a few seconds he sniffed round it warily, for Fred, being a champion, was an intelligent animal and poodles are intelligent dogs. Nevertheless canine intelligence has limitations while canine greed has none and before long he had started to eat the steak. At first he had done so slowly, savouring its succulence, but then he began to bolt it, scarcely chewing at all.

Two hours later the keenest kennelmaid, a stout pink girl named Rose, came walking briskly down the path and noticed a sleek black shape stretched out at the corner of one of the enclosures. In an instant she knew that it was the champion of Three Corners, the son of Champion Whately Winner and Champion Connemara Cutie and the finest dog ever bred in Ailsa Potts' kennels. A few seconds later she was inside the cage, kneeling beside him. He was, of course, extremely dead.

1

Ailsa Potts had been in poodles all her adult life. She'd toyed with Yorkshire terriers just after the war and in the early fifties had been duped into promoting the introduction of Irish water spaniels. Throughout both experiments she had remained loyal to the poodle, particularly to the full-size variety, which, as she constantly told everybody, she regarded as more 'virile' than its diminutive forms.

On the morning of the death of Champion Whately Wonderful Mrs Potts had porridge for breakfast. Porridge followed by bacon and egg and sausage, followed by thick slices of toast and butter and dollops of sweet, transparent marmalade. Mrs Potts had the reputation, throughout the canine world, of being a 'fine trencherwoman' and a 'good doer'. As a consequence she was quite remarkably fat and had grown fatter with the meals. She had little time for clothes and cared nothing for her personal appearance. As a result she never seemed to meet in the middle, for the grey skirts and pastel cardigans which constituted the whole of her wardrobe had been bought years before when she was under twelve stones. Safety pins held the cardigans together under her gigantic, drooping bosom and more safety pins aided her skirts. Where the holes had appeared in her garments she had occasionally sewed a large button, though more often she left them. Recently as the skirts were becoming impossible she had purchased two pairs of dark brown corduroy trousers which she tied at the waist with string. Once upon a time she had been pretty, in a cuddly way, and hidden among the folds of flesh and under the piles of sloppily applied face powder you could still see it. But it had been a long time ago.

That morning she was consuming her third piece of toast and was brewing up a second tea-bag when a hysterical kennelmaid rushed into the room.

'It's Fred,' she cried, 'Fred's dead.'

Mrs Potts had a mouthful of toast and marmalade and a handful of teacup. For a moment mouth and hand remained immobile. Then, slowly, she swallowed the toast and replaced the cup.

'What?' she said.

The kennelmaid was weeping noisily and uncontrollably. Mrs Potts got up, wiped crumbs from her wobbling chin and walked to the corner cupboard. From it she produced a bottle of Grand Seigneur ten star brandy and poured two fingers into a china cup.

'Drink that, girl,' she said, forcing it down the maid's mouth. The maid coughed extravagantly but stopped crying. Mrs Potts poured another measure of Grand Seigneur into the cup and drank it herself. Then she lit a cigarette.

'Now. What did you say?'

'Fred. He's dead.'

Mrs Potts exhaled.

'I was afraid that was what you said.' She sat quite still for five seconds and momentarily it seemed that the fat face might pucker into distress as uncontrolled as the kennelmaid's. Instead she took another drag at the cigarette and brushed the suspicion of a tear from her left eye.

'We'd better have a look then.'

It was sunny outside but still chill. There was a heavy dew. Mrs Potts, strapped uncomfortably into a navy blue duffel coat, walked purposefully down the asphalt path, striking out at encroaching nettles with her stick.

Rose, tears still streaking her cheeks, followed a few strides behind. The kennels were fifty yards from the house, on the other side of a patch of wasteland which had once been a herbaceous bordered lawn. Mrs Potts walked through the gates and glanced unseeing at the dogs who came running to the front of their cages to wag good morning. Instead she walked on to the far corner where, in the Number One kennel, Whately Wonderful had lived.

Two kennelmaids were standing in grubby brown overalls staring down at the dead dog. They were doing nothing but stare. Mrs Potts spoke sharply.

'No use crying over spilt milk,' she said. 'There's still work to do. You're not buttering parsnips like that. You too, Rose.'

When they'd gone back to routine, Mrs Potts knelt down beside Fred's body. He was very obviously dead. His jaws sagged open and his eyes gazed blankly into the distance. Mrs Potts shut them with unexpected gentleness and then picked up his left front paw. For fully a minute she held it in her hands, then she let it fall back on to the earth. She stood and dusted herself down, her face settling into an expression of resolution.

'Rose,' she shouted.

Rose came running.

'We'll bury him after lunch,' she said with a crispness which did not entirely conceal her true feelings. 'Use a dustbin liner and then find a good strong box. No cardboard this time. And get Andrews to dig a grave under the cherry tree.'

'Yes, Mrs Potts,' said Rose. Then, nervously, she said, 'Straight away, Mrs Potts? I mean shouldn't Mr Agnew . . . ?'

Mr Agnew was the vet. He came to the kennels most days to advise and inoculate and examine, and most of all to drink gin and water.

'No need for Mr Agnew,' said Mrs Potts, 'the dog's dead. And I know what caused it.' She grimaced. 'I'd rather Mr Agnew didn't know anything about it, so don't go gossiping.'

Simon Bognor was not happy with his latest assignment. There was nothing unusual in this since he had never yet been happy with his latest assignment. Nevertheless in a career which had taken him to an Anglican Friary in pursuit of missing industrial secrets, to stately homes in search of titled murderers and to the gossip column of a national newspaper to find the identity of the columnist's assassin, this took the biscuit. He grinned wanly. 'Taking the biscuit' was an unfortunate turn of phrase in view of the task before him.

Parkinson, his immediate superior in the Special Investigations Department at the Board of Trade, had tried to impress him with the seriousness of this situation but he hadn't succeeded.

It was not the first time that Bognor had wondered what he was doing with his life. He wondered about it daily, sometimes hourly, and invariably he came to the conclusion that he was wasting it. Ever since the interview at Oxford when he had foolishly allowed himself to be deflected from a sensible, routine application for some Civil Service posting into what was laughingly called 'intelligence'; ever since then things had gone wrong. He wasn't cut out for it, and his superiors, realizing this, had not, as they should have done, asked for him to be transferred or even sacked. Instead they had fobbed him off with absurdities in the hope that he would thus stay out of trouble. Alas, it meant no such thing. The more absurd and low-key his assignment, the more trouble he attracted.

He had an uneasy feeling that this would be the same.

'Dogs,' Parkinson had said. 'Know anything about dogs?'

'Very little.' Bognor didn't care for them since, as a child, he had been bitten on the hand by a stray in Richmond Park. They alarmed him—even chihuahuas

—and he had been known to kick out at perfectly inoffensive animals when the owners weren't looking.

'Never mind.' Parkinson had been unnervingly friendly. 'This could be your chance.' He had referred to the open file on his desk. 'Dogs are very big dollar earners. We make the best in the world, set very high standards. Total export income from dogs is more than two million pounds a year. Did you know that, Bognor?'

Bognor had not known.

'British dog breeders send more than two thousand Yorkshire terriers abroad every year. Are you impressed, Bognor?'

Bognor was very impressed. Also apprehensive. He thought he could see what was coming.

'So you will understand that the Board of Trade is surprisingly interested in man's best friend,' Parkinson had continued. He had droned on a bit about the place of the dog industry in Britain's balance of payments crisis and then stopped.

'Heard of quarantine?' he asked.

Bognor had said something facetious about chickenpox. Parkinson was not amused. Very patiently he had explained to Bognor that rabies was endemic in every other country in Europe and most other countries in the world except for Australia and New Zealand. To prevent it being imported all dogs coming in to Britain had to spend six months in quarantine kennels. Bognor nodded. He was getting worried.

'Now.' Parkinson was approaching the nitty gritty. 'These quarantine restrictions mean that it is not possible to fly dogs in and out of the country for very short periods. Right?'

'Right.'

'So that if a breeder wanted to put one of his dogs in for a show in Tokyo or Los Angeles he would have to kennel the dog when it returned. The same if he wanted to mate the dog with a Peruvian or Australian bitch.'

Bognor had frowned and Parkinson, very patiently,

explained what was going on. According to the Board of Trade's information an international gang was smuggling pedigree dogs in and out of Britain. They were appearing at foreign shows under assumed names and carrying off all the big prizes. They were being mated with foreign dogs for improbably high stud fees. And at no time were any of them going into quarantine.

'What makes you think this?'

Parkinson laughed. 'Our experts have reported an unusual rise in the standard of some breeds in some exceptionally unlikely places. Best of Breed boxer at Moscow this year,' he shuffled through papers, 'was quite exceptional. In my opinion only one kennel in the world could have produced such a dog, and that is in Lincolnshire. Then there was a Dobermann in Darjeeling and a Sealyham in Sydney. Exactly the same. Our man insists that those dogs could not have been produced by any breeder operating in that country, let alone the one who claims to have produced it. The latest is a Tibetan terrier in Tokyo. That was last week.'

Now sucking his pencil in the scruffy subterranean office off Whitehall Bognor pondered the fate which ordained that he should investigate a team of international dog smugglers. He was not amused, but it could have been worse. For a hideous moment he had feared that Parkinson was going to make him impersonate a dog breeder. Worse things had happened in the past, but to his intense relief he had only told him to get in touch with the Board of Trade's informant, a man called Mervyn Sparks.

For the last thirty minutes Bognor had been sucking the pencil and staring sadly at the telephone. He knew that soon he would have to stir himself and dial the wretched Sparks but somehow he could not yet bring himself to do so. Sparks was an international dog judge who had once bred Airedales but had stopped when the breed had lost popularity after the war. He had his own public relations consultancy and had worked in wartime intelligence, hence his continuing, if tenuous, links with the Civil Service.

Bognor was on the verge of picking up the receiver when the phone rang, making him jump.

'Bognor,' he said.

'Ah, Mr Bognor,' said the voice in the machine, 'Mervyn Sparks here. I wonder if you'd care to lunch. I think I may be able to help in your latest investigation. Mr Parkinson tells me you're in charge.'

'Ah. Yes. Thanks.'

'I have an appointment at two, so if you don't mind an early bite perhaps you'd meet me at the Club at 12.30.'

'The Club?'

'The Kennel Club. Clarges Street.'

'Oh. Yes. Fine.'

Bognor did not want lunch at the Kennel Club and disliked eating before 1.30. Nevertheless duty was clearly beckoning. He sighed and went on sucking his pencil.

Mr Sparks was shuffling testily up and down just inside the front door of his club when Bognor arrived at 12.31. Bognor apologized for being late and remarked approvingly on the large canine bronze which stood at the entrance.

'Nice dog,' he said fatuously.

'Not a dog,' said Mr Sparks acidly. 'It's a hound.'

Bognor was about to ask the difference and then thought better of it. They ascended by lift, in silence.

They went straight into lunch since time pressed and for the same reason ordered from the set menu which, Bognor noticed, was extremely modestly priced. Mr Sparks had the face of a weasel and drank a glass of cider with his lunch. Bognor would have preferred wine but did the same. Over the soup Mr Sparks, who had hitherto confined himself to curt banalities, leant across the table and said, 'I've just heard something very remarkable which might just be relevant.'

'Oh.' Bognor felt put upon. He was certainly not going to display enthusiasm without due cause.

'Whately Wonderful's been found dead.'

For a moment Bognor thought of trying to bluff his way out of this inexplicable revelation but instead he looked what he felt: totally blank.

'I'm awfully sorry,' he said. 'You'll have to explain. It means nothing.'

Mr Sparks sipped cider and looked wary.

'Whately Wonderful,' he hissed, 'dead.'

'I heard you perfectly clearly. I just don't understand. I've never heard of anyone called Whately Wonderful.'

'It's not a person, it's a dog.'

Bognor despaired. He didn't even seem able to identify breeds correctly.

'I'm sorry,' he said, 'I'm afraid I don't know anything at all about dogs. I was only assigned to this thing this morning.'

Mr Sparks looked pained and his rodent's mouth twitched in disapproval. 'That,' he said, 'is becoming obvious. I shall start at the beginning. You've heard of Ailsa Potts?'

'No.'

'I really am tempted to ask where you have been all these years, Mr Bognor, I am really. Mrs Potts is the country's, probably the world's, leading breeder of poodles.'

'Ah.'

'And she owns—or rather owned—a young dog called Whately Wonderful which by all accounts is the finest poodle ever bred. A superb creature. Magnificent animal. She'd already been offered £15 000 for it.'

'£15 000?'

'That's a top price but not so remarkable these days. She wouldn't sell for that, of course, and quite right. The dog's worth far more to her.'

'How so?'

'It was an almost certain Best of Breed for Cruft's and it had a better than even chance of becoming Best in Show. That would have put its own price up and also inundated her with orders from all over the world. She could have sold any dog she had several times over. Albert Ramble would have gone berserk.'

'Albert Ramble?'

They were on to their steak and kidney pie now. Mr Sparks was having difficulty with a piece of gristle. Eventually when he'd extracted it from his teeth and put it neatly on one side of his plate he said, 'Ailsa Potts' old rival. The second best breeder of poodles in Britain. He tries harder but then he has to. Nice man but doesn't quite have what it takes. His dogs are never as well bodied up as the Three Corners' animals. The ribbing's not good enough.'

'And the dog's dead.'

'Yes. This morning. One of the kennelmaids telephoned.' Mr Sparks tapped his nose suggestively with an ill-kempt finger. 'I have to keep up to date, know what's going on. That sort of thing.'

'And you think this dog's death might have something to do with the smuggling?'

Mr Sparks looked evasive.

'I can't be certain, but it's a peculiar coincidence. The circumstances are highly suspicious. I understand Mrs Potts wouldn't have the vet in. The dog was being buried this afternoon with no post mortem.'

Bognor was on the point of asking whether there didn't have to be an inquest and then realized that the question would be thought facetious. Instead he asked for Mrs Potts' address. For the first time since they'd met he'd asked Mr Sparks the right question. He scribbled down, 'Three Corners, Surblington' and Mr Sparks said he'd been hoping he'd go and have a word with Mrs Potts, whom he described as 'one of the old school', a phrase which filled Bognor with unreasoning horror.

During the ice cream they forgot the particular problem of Whately Wonderful to consider the more general one of dog smuggling. Sparks was only moderately helpful. On his travels he had recently encountered several high class dogs that he suspected of being from leading British kennels, but he couldn't prove it. It remained a suspicion. He hadn't seen any British dog breeders except occasionally for one or other who had been invited, like him, to judge. The only man who got around as much as he himself was his fellow judge, Percy Pocklington, the general secretary of the Doglovers' League. He didn't like Pocklington but, well, dog didn't bite dog, and he didn't want to speak ill of anyone who had done so much for dogdom.

Bognor said he'd never believed the aphorism about dogs not biting other dogs. In any case wasn't it 'eating' not 'biting'?

Mr Sparks wasn't interested in semantics. It was 1.30. Surblington was not much more than half an hour if the traffic was fair.

'You suggest,' he said, trying against every inclination to appear ingratiating, 'that I should see Mrs Potts about her dead dog; and also grill Percy Pocklington.'

'Yes.'

'In that case I shall take your advice.'

Mr Sparks acknowledged the tribute with a thin, humourless smile.

'Tell me,' asked Bognor, disliking the smile, 'why aren't there any dogs here? I mean, surely it's more appropriate for dogs to be members of the Kennel Club than their masters. I haven't seen a single dog—or hound since we arrived.'

Mr Sparks picked up the bill.

'It was good of you to come, Mr Bognor,' he said. 'I trust I've been of assistance. My regards to Mrs Potts.'

Bognor drove aggressively to Shepherd's Bush and then fast down the A40, his progress slowed only by the interminable roundabouts which interrupted his progress every few miles. Past Northolt airport he touched 80 mph which was too fast both for him and his little Mini. He only ever drove like that when he was angry. It was the unpleasant little informer who'd upset him. Mr Sparks had reminded him of the school sneak.

However, in this sort of work people like him were tedious and disagreeable necessities. He slowed down. There was no hurry. Mrs Potts was not expecting him because he hadn't telephoned. He had thought it better to surprise her, though quite why he didn't know. At the back of his mind there was the feeling that if he'd asked to see her she would have turned him down.

He found the kennels without trouble. There was a large sign on the main road into Surblington which said 'Three Corners Kennels—Standard and Miniature Poodles—Boarding. Mrs M. Potts'. Bognor parked the car by driving half-way up the grass verge which ran to the privet hedge. Then he walked to the front door of the dilapidated Victorian villa, brushed aside the honey-suckle which hung limply around the front door and rang the bell. He waited, an unlikely caller for a dog breeder, he reckoned. Normally he would have dressed the part but that morning when he left the flat there had been no question of anything to do with dogs. More likely codes, ciphers, the odd check on the activities of the Iron Curtain trade councillors. Perhaps a straight-forward piece of suspected industrial sabotage if he'd been really lucky. Because of this he was still in his charcoal suit. It was bagging slightly at the knees, shining slightly at the elbows, thinning slightly at the cuffs but it was still unmistakably a city suit. He smoothed the back of his head and grimaced at the sparseness of the hair there. Still a few years before he was forty. He must take up squash again. It might not make his hair grow but it would get rid of his paunch. He rang the doorbell again and stepped back to take a look round.

The house was a shambles. It badly needed re-paint-ing and the paint was flaking everywhere. On the first floor a window had been broken and the pane had been replaced with corrugated brown paper. Several tiles were missing from the roof and one of the drain-pipes had come away from the wall. Bognor could smell drains. He sighed and thought of lighting a che-root. Cheroots were a new pastime and they affected his breath which was becoming alarmingly short. Mon-

ica disapproved. Suddenly as he stood gazing up at the
headquarters of Britain's poodle breeding industry he
became aware of an alien noise. He strained to identify it. It appeared to be coming from behind the
house. He walked round to the back and was rewarded
by an increase in volume. It was singing. Very poor
singing, high pitched, querulous, dirge-like. He advanced on its source which seemed to be the orchard
to the right of what he now recognized as a kennel
block. He traversed the wasteland listening hard now
to identify the sounds. Unless he was much mistaken
it was 'Abide with me' sung by a small choir of tone-
deaf ladies. One had a dominating soprano and somewhere in the middle of it all there was a cracked bass.
He continued his advance and noticed that the orchard
could only be entered through a wrought iron gate of
surprisingly ornate design. Over the top of it, picked out
in faded gilt were the words:

> *The kiss of the sun for pardon,*
> *The song of the birds for mirth.*
> *You are nearer God's heart in a garden,*
> *Than anywhere else on earth.*

It was undoubtedly 'Abide with me'. The singing was
execrable but the tune was recognizable if only because
the human voices were augmented by some dim and
crackling organ music. Bognor pushed open the gate
and was amazed.

Twenty-five yards away under a cherry tree of perfect symmetry stood a small group. Three were in overalls with black armbands. One, a lady of considerable
bulk, sported an enormous black hat, and a fifth seemed
incongruous—snappily dressed in a camel trouser suit,
and with long blonde hair flowing over her shoulders.
The only man in the group was an elderly agricultural
type in heavy boots and braces. He was standing firmly
to attention with a cloth cap clasped over his heart. At
his feet lay a large wooden box, which Bognor saw as
he drew closer had the words 'Outspan Oranges—with

care' stencilled over it. He had been right about the organ music too. It came from a hand-operated gramophone which had been placed on an upright dining-room chair a little to the right of the tree. By some curious inbred reflex Bognor began to tiptoe. As he did the singing stopped and the blonde glanced in his direction. She noticed him and smiled. Bognor wished he hadn't worn such an old suit. He felt as if he was playing grandmother's footsteps and as he had arrived within a few feet of the group he decided to stay where he was.

The fat lady in the hat, whom he guessed from her shape and demeanour to be Mrs Potts herself, now stepped to the edge of the hole in the ground and, in a voice breaking with emotion, recited:

> *'In life the firmest friend;*
> *The first to welcome, foremost to defend;*
> *Whose honest heart is still his master's own,*
> *Who labours, fights, lives, breathes for him alone.'*

Bognor was appalled at the use to which Byron had been put. Lines completed, Mrs Potts signalled to the gardener, who manhandled the orange box clumsily into the hole. This done she produced a large yellow handkerchief and said, barely audibly, 'Goodbye, Fred. You were a lovely dog,' then she subsided snivelling into the folds of the handkerchief as the gardener began to shovel earth on the grave. Bognor who felt that he had intruded unforgivably into this scene of private grief hurried back to the wrought iron gate to await the return of the mourners. On his way he noticed several small tombstones, many of them inscribed. 'In happy memory of my old mate, Bonzo Eglington', said one, while another, more grandly, proclaimed: 'Bolislav—a very gallant dog'.

It was several minutes before the women returned. The gardener had evidently been left behind to finish his job. What other bizarre rites had been performed Bognor could only guess. The three girls in overalls

—one of them presumably Mervyn Sparks' informant—came first, fresh-faced and looking relieved that the ordeal was over. Mrs Potts and the blonde followed a few paces behind, the younger woman arming the breeder along. As they came to the gate he emerged in a manner which he recognized as being absurdly theatrical but which seemed at the time the only way possible.

'Mrs Potts, I presume,' he said. 'Allow me to introduce myself. Bognor of the Board of Trade. I apologize for intruding at a moment of personal distress but . . .'

He seemed to come as a shock to Mrs Potts, who drew back in alarm and failed to accept his proffered hand. She had obviously not noticed him earlier. Her face was an unsightly mess of tear-stains and stale make-up. Luckily the blonde was under control. She smiled conspiratorially.

'I'm Coriander Cordingley,' she said, taking Bognor's hand and holding it for an instant longer than etiquette required. 'Mrs Potts has had rather a shock and I was going to make her a cup of tea. Perhaps you'd join us.'

'Thank you.' Bognor fell into step—or rather shuffle—alongside them.

'Did you say Board of Trade?' asked Miss Cordingley, brightly. She was about thirty, Bognor guessed, and was wearing almost enough make-up to make her look prostitutional. Almost but not quite. 'Yes,' he said.

'How frightfully interesting.'

'Oh.' Bognor was perplexed. Nobody ever said that about his job. Then before he realized that she was simply being polite he said, 'What makes you say that?'

She blushed slightly. 'You must meet such interesting people.' Bognor guessed she said that to everyone.

'Yes, of course,' he said, 'frightfully interesting.'

She laughed.

They had reached the house now and they went in through the back door. The kitchen smelt of rancid fat and bacon rinds. Bognor wrinkled his nose and was pleased to see that Coriander Cordingley did the same.

Mrs Potts who had been immersed in lachrymose silence since Bognor's introduction suddenly became galvanized. She strode to a cake tin surrounded by half-empty jam jars on the sideboard, opened it and removed three-quarters of a Battenburg cake spotted with green mould. This she deposited on a cracked willow pattern plate together with the remains of a packet of Garibaldi biscuits. From the hooks above the cake tin she took three cups, chipped, stained with lipstick and with tidemarks of tea clearly visible an inch below the rim.

'Would you like tea?' she asked. 'Or would a drink be better?'

'A drink,' said Bognor too eagerly, and was relieved when Miss Cordingley said the same.

'Bravo,' responded Mrs Potts, now much restored. Bognor was upset to see that she did not replace the filthy teacups. Instead she went to the stove, opened the oven and peered in.

'Scotch, brandy or tonic wine,' she said.

Bognor opted for whisky while the two women had brandy. The brandy was the same brand that had been administered that morning—Grand Seigneur ten star—while Bognor's whisky was poured from a bottle marked 'McCrum's guaranteed ten-year-old whisky' and subtitled 'purveyors of Scottish Whisky to His Majesty the King of Nepal'.

'More comfortable next door,' said Mrs Potts, taking the comestibles in one hand, her drink in the other and pushing the door open with her bottom. They followed her into a dingy drawing room, darkened by yellowing net curtains and ornamented with large numbers of silver cups. There were photographs everywhere, nearly all of poodles. On an upright piano, however, Bognor noticed one of a statuesque woman in a fox fur and fruit salad hat, standing next to a slight man with a Clark Gable moustache and spats. With a start Bognor realized that the picture was of a younger Mrs Potts with, presumably, Mr Potts. He sat down gingerly on the edge of a fragile Victorian chair with an anti-

macassar, declining his hostess's offer of Garibaldi or
Battenburg and watched fascinated, as she carved herself a portion consisting of almost half the remaining
mildewed cake.

'Well,' said Mrs Potts, 'as I said, Coriander, I'm
afraid I've no one else for you to paint. I'll pay you, of
course.'

'Oh nonsense, Mrs Potts,' said Miss Cordingley, 'I
wouldn't dream of it. As soon as you have another dog
like Fred just let me know and I'll be down in a flash.'

'There'll never be another dog like Fred,' said Mrs
Potts morosely, 'he was unique. Not while I live there
won't be anyway.' She took a mouthful of cake and a
noisy slug of Grand Seigneur. 'Now, young man,' she
turned to address Bognor, who was duly flattered. It
was a long time since anyone had called him a young
man. The woman was still, he supposed, blinded by
grief. 'What can we do for you? I'm afraid you've
found us at a sad moment. You may not realize it but
that's not just a dog I've lost, it's my future. I could
have retired on the proceeds of that dog. He was a
friend, too, I know, but he was worth a thousand times
his weight in gold, make no mistake.'

'What about the insurance?' asked Bognor, trained
against his true nature to be suspicious at all times.

'Pshaw,' said Mrs Potts waving dismissive fingers,
thick as bananas. She drained her cup and went out
of the room.

'Do you paint . . . er . . . dogs?' asked Bognor, smiling at Miss Cordingley.

'Yes.'

'Is that lucrative?'

'You'd be surprised,' she said. 'Not so much the
money, but the travel and the expenses. I've been all
over the world painting dogs.'

'Do you like dogs?'

She made a face. Mrs Potts returned with the Grand
Seigneur and the McCrum's. Without asking she refilled
all their cups.

'Well,' repeated Mrs Potts. 'You don't look as if

you've come to buy a dog. I should say you're more of a cat person. Or even a parrot person. Do you keep parrots?'

Bognor shook his head. 'I'm here on business,' he said.

'Let me guess,' said Mrs Potts. 'It can't be the licence. I've done that. And it wouldn't be the car. Is it the VAT?'

'No,' said Bognor, 'it's about dogs. As a matter of fact it's about Whately Wonderful.'

For a moment she had seemed slightly tipsy. Now she was sober again, and very on edge.

"What do you mean?"

'I heard the dog was dead . . .'

'How? No one else knew. It only happened this morning. How could you possibly . . . ?'

'We at the Board of Trade . . .' Bognor was about to launch into his long and frankly pompous spiel about the all-seeing intelligence network at the Board's disposal, but Mrs Potts prevented him.

'That bloody kennelmaid,' she said explosively, 'I'll have her for this. I told the little bitch to keep her trap shut.' She drank more brandy and Bognor realized that although she was upset about the dog there was more to it than that. She was frightened.

'It doesn't honestly matter how I knew,' he said, gently, 'and it may be irrelevant. The point is, you see, that I'm investigating a dog smuggling business and my informant suggested that there might possibly be some connection between the sudden death of your dog and . . .'

'Don't be ridiculous,' she snapped at him. 'How the hell could there be? What are you talking about?'

'All right,' said Bognor, 'I admit it seems far-fetched. But I wonder if you'd mind telling me precisely what it was your dog died of? I understand he was a young healthy dog. Isn't it rather unusual for a dog like that to suddenly drop dead?'

'Not at all,' said Mrs Potts. 'The dog just died and that's all there is to it. It was a virus.'

'What sort of virus?'

'You obviously don't know the first thing about dogs. It could have been any sort of virus.' Bognor knew she was bluffing. He might not know anything about dogs but he had acquired a certain knowledge of human nature.

'What exactly did the vet say?'

'Nothing.'

'Oh?'

'The vet wasn't called. As far as I'm concerned the vet's job is to look after live dogs and keep them healthy. Once a dog's dead it's of no interest to him and he's of no use to it.'

Bognor sighed. He wished he knew more about dogs.

'Isn't it usual to call the vet if a dog dies in these circumstances?'

'I don't know why you're being so suggestive. There weren't any "circumstances". The dog died. No, I don't call in the vet when a dog dies. I see no reason for it.'

He was stymied.

'I'm sorry,' he said. 'Was the dog insured?'

She bridled. Whether it was because of real annoyance or whether it was part of her act he couldn't be sure.

'Do you have any authority for asking these questions?'

He produced his ID card and she examined it suspiciously, turning it over a couple of times and screwing her eyes up to read the small print.

'That doesn't give you any authority,' she said eventually, 'it just says who you are. What do you think, Coriander?' She passed the card across to Miss Cordingley who glanced at it and said with the tone of one who doesn't expect her advice to be contradicted: 'It doesn't give Mr Bognor any authority, Ailsa, but in view of who he is and who he works for I think it might be nice to help.'

Mrs Potts appeared to consider. Bognor was grateful to Coriander. He had almost forgotten she was there. She'd been very quiet while he was interrogating.

Eventually Mrs Potts appeared to concede. 'All right,' she said, 'I'll help in any way I can, but I really don't see what connection there can possibly be between Fred and this smuggling nonsense.'

Bognor smiled ingratiatingly. Mrs Potts, who had polished off the whole of the Battenburg cake, began to make inroads on the Garibaldis. She was undoubtedly agitated.

'For a start,' he said, 'is this smuggling thing feasible? For instance, if you could have taken Whately Wonderful to foreign dog shows or mated him with foreign dogs, would that have made much difference to you financially?'

'Yes.'

'But it wouldn't be practical?'

'No.'

'Why not?'

'Quarantine mainly. But other countries have their own regulations.'

'Have you heard anyone mention anything about a smuggling ring like this? No one's approached you, for instance?'

Bognor was aware of hesitation. The two women didn't even look at one another, but he was certain that something passed between them. What? He couldn't be sure. He wasn't psychic, but there was something there.

It was Coriander who answered. 'As I said, I travel about an awful lot,' she said, 'and I just don't see how it could be done. Customs are awfully strict.'

'If you can smuggle arms and illegal immigrants you can presumably smuggle dogs. I mean you can put little dogs into handbags.'

'Oh really, Mr Bognor, I thought you were being serious.' Miss Cordingley laughed patronizingly.

'But neither of you have ever heard of it happening?' They both shook their heads.

'I've sold abroad,' said Mrs Potts. 'The best dog I ever had, apart from Fred, went to a Count in Florence. He paid £3000 and never showed him. Nor bred from him either. Just took him round the town to show off to his mistresses and his wife's lovers.'

Bognor finished his whisky. It was obvious to him that they were both lying and that he wasn't going to get any further that day. He continued to ask questions in a perfunctory manner, neither expecting nor obtaining any satisfactory answers. After five minutes he rose to leave.

'Can I offer you a lift?' he said to Coriander.

She smiled. 'It's very kind of you, but I have a return ticket and Ailsa and I still have a few things to talk about. But if I can help . . . ' She took a card from her handbag. 'Let's meet for a drink. I really think you're wasting your time, but the drink would be nice anyway.' Once more she held his hand a fraction longer than necessary.

Mrs Potts was more abrupt.

'Next time you come,' she said, 'I hope it will be to buy a poodle. Can't afford to fiddle about with tomfool stories about smuggling.' He hardly listened, mesmerized instead by the crumb of marzipan which had stuck to her chin.

2

He was early back to the flat and there was no sign of
Monica. They had lived together for as long as he cared
to remember now and their routines were at least as
established as those of most married couples. He seldom
returned before 6.30. She was always there to greet
him, but had usually only been home for a few minutes.
She took jobs when and where she felt like it, but always made a point of being out in the afternoons. He
supposed that one day they would marry but somehow
with time and familiarity the prospect receded rather
than advanced.

The view over Regent's Park was idyllic on an early
summer's day like this. All leaves were lime green with
youth, untainted with age or city grime. He stood for a
moment looking south, then went to the kitchen to make
coffee, forgetting, briefly, the tedious business of dogs.
After the kettle had boiled and he'd spooned into a cup
one and a half teaspoons of brown granules he took the
resulting concoction to the drawing room and sprawled
full length on the faded sofa. It was nice to be able to
put one's feet up. He sipped at the steaming liquid and
perused the last edition of the evening paper. There had
been an armed bank robbery in a suburban high street
and the President of the United States had told another
lie. The stock market had had a bad day and so had the
English cricket team. Nothing ever changed. He turned
to the back page where the home news stories lived and

23

immediately read a headline which set the adrenalin flowing.

'Duchess in Rabies Scare' was the headline. The story underneath was simple. 'An outbreak of rabies is feared at the home of Dora, Duchess of Dorset, following the death there of one of the Duchess's Dandie Dinmont terriers. A spokesman for the Duchess confirmed that the dog, Champion Piddlehampton Peter, had been destroyed early today after apparently going berserk and attacking one of the Duchess's kennelmaids. The spokesman refused to comment on the suggestion that rabies could be involved but local medical authorities have appealed to all those who may have been in contact with the kennels to come forward for anti-rabies injections.'

There followed a note from 'Our Medical Correspondent' describing the inexorable agonies of death from hydrophobia, and emphasizing that unless injections were given soon after a bite from a rabid dog, the disease was virtually incurable. Under that there was another note from 'Our Pets Correspondent' giving a brief résumé of the quarantine restrictions and referring to the last outbreak of rabies, in Camberley. And finally 'Our Social Correspondent' appended a note about the Duchess—the Dowager Duchess—who had bred Dandie Dinmonts for more than twenty years with enormous success. She had also at an earlier stage in her career piloted a Sopwith Camel under Clifton Suspension Bridge and won a hundred guineas by dancing naked round the pond in the middle of Tom Quad, Christchurch, during the Commem Ball of 1921.

Bognor was suitably appalled. Rabies, he now knew, could only be imported from abroad and it could only be passed on by animals—particularly dogs. That meant one of three things. First that the Duchess of Dorset had imported a Dandie Dinmont and somehow the quarantine restrictions had proved inadequate. That had happened in the Camberley case. The rabid dog had actually been in quarantine kennels approved by the Ministry but the period had not been long enough.

Regulations had now been tightened but it was conceivable that something of the sort might have happened. The second possibility was that the kennels had been visited—unknown to them—by a rabid visitor, or by an animal capable of carrying the disease. Both of these exempted the Duchess from any blame, but the third was bad. It seemed most likely to Bognor that the Duchess's dog had contracted the disease abroad and somehow returned home without going into kennels for the statutory period. That made the Duchess not only blameworthy but criminally liable, too. He stood up and began pacing the room. Could there be any connection between this death and that of Whately Wonderful and if so what? Had Whately Wonderful died of rabies? He wondered if, on the strength of his half-formulated suspicion, he could order the dog's exhumation and a post mortem. And if it had died from rabies what would it prove?

He was struggling with the ramifications of the case when the phone rang. Instinctively he knew that it would be Parkinson and that it would be bad news. Parkinson had never yet rung when there was good news to communicate. As usual he was right.

'I'm afraid I've got bad news for you, Bognor,' said Parkinson. Bognor gulped. It must indeed be bad news if Parkinson was prefacing it with a warning like that. He waited.

'It's about Mervyn Sparks.'

'I had lunch with him.'

'So I gather. He's in hospital now.'

'Christ. It's not food poisoning . . .' Bognor's instinct for self-preservation invariably got the better of him in moments of stress.

He could feel the exasperation in Parkinson's voice when he replied.

'I thought you might have realized what it might be. Haven't you read this evening's papers?'

'Yes, but . . .'

'He has rabies.'

'Good God. But how?'

'I've just come from the hospital. They let me talk to him briefly. He had been to the Duchess of Dorset's and he *was* bitten by one of her bloody dogs.'

'But surely he got an injection?'

'Not even anti-tetanus. Let alone a rabies jab. It was only a little bite. It never occurred to him.'

'But, good lord, he's supposed to be an expert.'

'Even experts are fallible. After all, if you were given a small nip by a terrier in the middle of Dorset you wouldn't assume you were about to contact rabies. This was Piddlehampton, not Karachi.'

'Is he going to be all right?'

'The doctors say he has a few more hours. No more. He's in intensive care now. There's nothing they can do.'

Bognor was silent, remembering his unpleasant lunch. He hadn't liked Mr Sparks in the least, and Mr Sparks clearly hadn't liked him. Even so.

'I'm sorry,' he said, unable to think of anything more appropriate. He *was* sorry too. Not quite as desolated as he might have been, but still sorry.

'What do you want me to do?'

Parkinson was abrupt. 'Get off your arse and get down to the Duchess's. Fast.'

Bognor thought for a moment. 'If it's all the same to you . . . sir,' he said, with a mixture of servility and insolence, 'I'd prefer to go via Surblington.'

'Where?' Parkinson was irritated, but less so when Bognor had told him of the day's events. 'Get the corpse dug up,' he said, 'and we'll have the bloody thing examined. If it *was* rabies the woman's in trouble.'

They exchanged goodbyes and Bognor went to make more coffee.

It was ten minutes before Monica arrived. She had got a temporary job helping a friend in a new art gallery and there had been a problem with some sculptures which had been missing for days before finally being located at Didcot.

'Dogs!' she said in dismay, when Bognor told her. 'Whatever next?' She put down a bulging string bag, filled with extravagant goodies from Robert Jackson and the Berwick Street Market, took off her scarf and shook out her hair in front of the glass. Bognor made comparisons with Coriander Cordingley. Monica had lost weight recently but she was showing her age. There were lines on the face where last year there had been none. Still she was undoubtedly much, much nicer than Coriander Cordingley, even if she was five years older and, Bognor had to face it, a little on the plain side.

'Aunt Flo used to breed borzois,' she said, combing out her hair. 'I got steak for tonight. Ghastly price. I hope you don't mind.'

'Aunt Flo. Borzois? They're the aristocratic looking ones with long noses, aren't they?'

'Yes.'

'But Aunt Flo was common looking with a little snub nose.'

'Well?'

'I thought dogs were supposed to look like their owners.'

'Don't be silly. Anyway it's the other way round. Can I have a drink?'

He mixed two gins and tonic, while telling her more.

'Don't you think you ought to have a rabies injection?' she asked when he'd finished.

'No one's bitten me.'

'You can get it from saliva, I think. Has anyone licked you?'

'Dog or person?'

'Dog, stupid. The worst you get from people is glandular fever.'

'No. Try to be serious for a minute. If Sparks dies— and it sounds as if he's going to—do you think they could charge the old Duchess with murder?'

Monica looked thoughtful.

'Not murder, but I wouldn't be surprised by manslaughter.'

'That's rather what I thought.'

They sat and stared into their drinks. They'd lived

in the flat for eight years now—at least Bognor had.
Monica had moved in by degrees and it was only in
the last few months that she'd finally given up the
pretence of a place of her own. It had grown shabby
recently, but the shabbiness made it comfortable.

'I wonder,' said Bognor, 'if the Duchess realized
the dog was rabid when it bit Sparks.'

'That would be murder,' said Monica.

'Yes,' he said, 'I think it would.'

First thing next morning he dropped into the local
surgery for an anti-typhoid and cholera injection. It
was a routine jab—a six-monthly precaution against
the exotic trip to typhoid-ridden tropics. A trip on
which, incidentally, Parkinson steadfastly refused to
send him.

Later, on his way to Surblington, he called at the
Kennel Club. Just inside the entrance, on the left, there
was a window marked 'Enquiries'. He showed his card
to the man behind it and as usual it produced the de-
sired effect. The man became almost obsequious.

'I'm afraid I have a curious request and it may take
up a lot of your time,' said Bognor. 'But I assure you
it is important. I know how busy you must be.'

The minion smiled and nodded. 'Anything I can do,
sir. I'm only too happy to oblige.'

'Good,' said Bognor, taking a deep breath and asking, 'I simply want to know if any Dandie Dinmont has
won a prize in a foreign dog show in the last few weeks.
And if you find one, could you establish as many details about it as possible—the name of the owner, the
name of the judge, the organizing committee, anything
at all.'

The Kennel Club man betrayed no reaction whatever. 'Dandie Dinmont,' he said slowly. 'I presume it
would have to be quite a big prize. Best of Show, I
mean. And a big show at that?'

'I should think so, yes.'

'I'll do what I can,' he said. 'We have thirty-five

foreign associates. I'll check through their latest reports and let you know.'

It was mid-morning before he reached Three Corners. The traffic was heavy and he had a lot on his mind. He wondered if Sparks had died in the night and what sort of welcome awaited him at the Duchess of Dorset's. Occasionally he remembered Coriander Cordingley. There was something slightly strange about her. He parked the car on the verge again and on getting out was immediately assailed by the smell of meat, cooking. From the kennels came a yelping which he judged to be the pre-prandial cries of hungry dogs. He accordingly walked straight to the kennels and was rewarded by the sight of Mrs Potts supervising the catering. Her three kennelmaids were dispensing dried biscuit and steaming meat. The biscuit came from a sack, the meat from a black, gravy-stained vat.

'Morning, Mrs Potts,' he said with a cheerfulness he did not feel. The stench was horrid. The voluminous dog breeder turned slowly and peered at him with mild hostility.

'Good morning, young man. It's feeding time.'

'So I see. What are they having?'

'Meat and biscuit. And seaweed.'

'Seaweed?'

'Seaweed. I'll be with you in a minute or two. Do you want to buy a poodle this time?'

He shook his head and watched as she waddled down the path between the kennels and runs. There was little consistency about the buildings which had obviously been erected at different times. Some were of wood, some of corrugated iron and some of concrete blocks. The size of the runs varied too. After studying them Bognor decided that this was due to the different size or number of dogs in each compartment. In some there was only one dog. When this was so it was usually a scrupulously groomed poodle, presumably the pride and property of Mrs Potts herself. In some runs, however, up to a dozen were closeted together but when

this happened the dogs were an assortment of breeds,
many of which Bognor did not recognize. These were
presumably outside dogs whose owners had left them
at Three Corners while they went on holiday.

All the animals were voraciously hungry, gulping
down the smelly meat and anaemic biscuit as if it were
steak and chips. Bognor suspected it was horsemeat
from the knacker's yard.

Eventually, when she'd finished dishing up, Mrs
Potts was able to give Bognor her undivided attention.
She seemed to have all the self-confidence her bulk
suggested but beneath it Bognor was not so certain.

'Not more of this smuggling nonsense, I hope,' she
said, a little too brightly.

'You've seen what's happened at the Duchess of
Dorset's?'

'I've read the newspapers. You don't expect me to
believe that, do you? How could one of Dora's Dandies get rabies?' Her face folded into an apology of a
smile which vanished as quickly as it had arrived. 'And
how am I connected with that anyway?'

Bognor shrugged. 'I can't be sure, but in the circumstances we can't take risks. Therefore I'm afraid I'm
going to have to ask you to have your corpse dug up.
We want to do a post mortem.'

'And what do you expect to find?'

'What caused its death.'

They were still standing in the middle of the kennel
area, Mrs Potts' feet wide apart, a heavy pail on one
elbow and her other hand resting where, on a con-
ventionally proportioned person, one might have found
a hip. Bognor glanced round at the dogs, still chewing
over the last of their feed.

'The rest of your animals look quite healthy,' he said.
'Funny that none of them have contracted poor Fred's
virus.'

'Fred was in a place of his own. Isolated.'

She was remarkably truculent. Bognor wondered if
he'd made a mistake. At the moment she didn't give
the impression of someone harbouring a guilty secret.

'Would you mind?'

'What?'

'Having the body exhumed.'

'You're wasting your time.'

'We'll see about that.'

'Do you have the authority? You're not Ministry of Agriculture. Or police.'

Bognor thought of bluffing but instead said, 'No. But I can get it if you force me.'

She shrugged and her whole body wobbled in the gesture of resignation.

'Carry on,' she said. 'Do you want to take him away with you?'

'Yes, please.'

Again she shrugged, then began to waddle up the path towards the house, calling out at regular intervals: 'Andrews . . . Andrews . . . Andrews.' After thirty seconds of this shouting, the elderly agriculturalist whom Bognor had seen at yesterday's funeral emerged from behind a potting shed, doing up his flies.

'Morning, M'm,' he said, embarrassed. 'Morning, sir.'

'Mr Bognor here,' said Mrs Potts, gesturing at Bognor dismissively, 'wants to take Whately Wonderful away for an examination. Would you please dig him up again.'

Andrews made a gesture of salute, returned to the potting shed, entered and re-emerged a minute later with a spade. The three of them set off in the direction of the cemetery.

'Do you always bury your dogs in such style?' asked Bognor as they passed through the gate with its gilt doggerel about God's heart and the garden.

'How would you put your friends to rest, Mr Bognor?' asked Mrs Potts.

They advanced on the cherry tree.

'How long has the cemetery been here?' he asked.

'Nineteen-thirty,' she said. 'I inherited it from Mavis Briggs-Percival, the missionary. She kept Pekes. She's buried there—over by the willow.'

Bognor wandered over to the willow which wept

lushly over a simple granite tombstone with Miss
Briggs-Percival's name chiselled on it and the three
letters RIP underneath. All around it were much smaller stones inscribed to Wan-Tu, Mao, Ping, Wang and
other similarly Pekinese names. Bognor wondered why
he found it peculiar.

Fred had not been buried very deeply and when he
returned to the cherry he found that Andrews was
already kneeling over a small hole and trying to ex-
tricate the coffin with his hands. After much grunting
and sweat he emerged triumphant, clutching a battered
cake tin decorated with a bundle of roses.

'I thought . . .' Bognor felt a mounting sensation of
desperation. He concentrated very hard indeed and
managed to conjure up a precise image of an orange
box lying on the turf with the motto 'Outspan Oranges
—with care' stencilled on it. There was no question of
it. When Fred had been buried yesterday he had been
in an orange box and now he was reduced to the size
of a cake tin.

'Yes, Mr Bognor, you thought what?'

Bognor stared at her, trying to work out whether
beneath the blubber there was a sinister Machiavellian
mind or a silly frightened old woman. He was unable
to decide.

'I thought Whately Wonderful was buried in an
orange box.'

'What can have given you that idea?'

'I saw it.'

'You are mistaken.'

'But I saw it. Yesterday. I was here. Remember?'

'I'm afraid you are quite mistaken. Ask Andrews.'

Andrews was dusting earth from the cake tin, and
wiping its lid with the tail of his shirt, which protruded
from his waist.

'Excuse me, Mr Andrews,' said Bognor, with the
growing diffidence of the hopelessly conned, 'but yesterday I quite definitely saw Whately Wonderful being
laid to rest in an orange box.'

The old man regarded him with blank brown eyes,

then suddenly focused them and said, ' 'Fraid not, sir. We buried un in a cake tin. This cake tin here.' And he tapped the top of the tin with his forefinger. Bognor turned back to the dog breeder.

'How in God's name do you fit a full-size poodle into a cake tin?' he asked, his voice rising.

'Mr Bognor, you are being indelicate. I hardly feel you would want to discuss the details of cremation if you were referring to one of your own loved ones.'

'Cremation?'

'Cremation.'

'But when? How? Why?'

'It is usual.' Mrs Potts seemed to gain self-possession as Bognor lost his own. 'It's more hygienic and it takes up less space. There is a very useful local firm which is prepared to accommodate us when their incinerator is not otherwise occupied.'

'But, Mrs Potts . . .' Bognor made one final appeal. 'You know perfectly well that when I was here yesterday you were burying your dog in a large orange box. So you must have had him cremated after I'd gone away. Now why did you do that?'

For a moment he thought she was going to capitulate and tell him something, but it passed in an instant; however, it was enough to confirm that she was lying. He wasn't insane after all.

'I'm sorry, Mr Bognor, I'm very busy. Will you please take Fred and go.'

Andrews held out the cake tin and Bognor took it ungraciously.

'Goodbye,' he said, 'we'll be in touch.' Then he stamped tetchily back to his car, put the earthly remains of Champion Whately Wonderful into the boot and accelerated towards Dorset. He knew the Board's analysts were clever but he doubted whether they would be able to detect rabies in a cake tin of dust. They would just have to try.

Piddlehampton Manor was in the Piddle Valley, less humorously but no more correctly known as the Trent

Valley, that pastoral area of central Dorset which gave birth to the Tolpuddle Martyrs. It took Bognor over three hours to drive to Blandford, modestly announced on its own signposts as 'an interesting Georgian town'. Then he took the Dorchester road and saw signs to Bryantspuddle, Affpuddle, Puddletown, Piddlehinton and Piddletrenthide. Dorset, he reflected, had the finest place names in the world.

Unhappily he had more on his mind than place names. Two miles beyond Blandford he finally succumbed to macabre curiosity and pulled in by a phone box. It was three o'clock and Parkinson would be back from lunch.

When he'd eventually succeeded in reversing the charges—a process which took longer than it should because the operator persisted in thinking he wanted a number in Bognor and refused to believe that that was his name, he found Parkinson gloomy and censorious.

'He died this morning,' he said, 'in great pain.'

'Did he say anything?'

'Nothing coherent. Anyway no one was allowed to see him except the staff. It's not pretty, rabies. He was raving.'

Bognor felt ill. He wondered if he should have had an injection against rabies as well as cholera and typhoid.

'There was just one thing.' Parkinson's voice was very crackly. 'The doctor says he kept on about being eager to do something. He couldn't work out what it was but this word "eager" kept cropping up. The doctor couldn't work it out. I don't suppose it's important but I pass it on in the slender hope that you might be able to make something of it.'

Bognor caught sight of himself in the cracked glass of the phone booth's mirror. He saw a face on the verge of decay. Perhaps it wasn't too late to start a career as a schoolmaster.

'Doesn't make any sense to me,' he said.

'That doesn't mean it isn't important.' Parkinson's

voice had taken on its usual note of irritation. Bognor derived comfort from it.

'I'm afraid I had a rather abortive experience at Three Corners.'

'Can't hear. It's a bad line. Three what?'

'Three Corners. That dog. They've cremated it.'

'Do you have the ashes?'

'In a cake tin, in the boot.'

'When are you coming back?'

'Tonight, I hope.'

'Bring them back with you then. They can manage ashes all right. Why did they cremate him?'

'Don't know.'

There was a long pause. When he did speak again Parkinson sounded almost solicitous. 'For once in your life, Bognor, try to be careful. I have a nasty feeling this business is not as banal as it may seem.'

'Thanks for the thought.' Bognor hung up.

He reached Piddlehampton after another half hour of dreamy driving. Two dead dogs and now a dead man, he kept repeating to himself. Each one could be quite accidental, and yet . . .

The village was almost a parody. Its main, indeed its only, street wound gently up the hillside through two lines of thatched cottages set back behind well-mown grass verges. Roses burgeoned round tiny porches, climbed hungrily up to the roofs and clambered over garden walls. Half-way up the street a small Victorian almshouse stood opposite a neat Jacobean church which adjoined a perfect Georgian Rectory. All three periods blended happily in yellow stone. Only the twee anachronism of the Gothic script above Piddlehampton Post Office and General Stores jarred. The village seemed empty. The only sound was of pigeons cooing persistently and a hand-driven lawn mower clattering behind one of the cottages. Otherwise it might have been siesta time.

He drove through the village drinking in the peace of it all and followed the road for another half mile through woodland until, just round a sharp left-handed bend, he came to a lodge gate. The lodge itself, a stone single-storey building, was dilapidated and unlived in. The drive, which had once been gravel, was now a mess of pebbles and weeds, and singing gently from a peeling white post was a sign which said, 'Piddlehampton Pedigree Dandie Dinmonts—Manor Kennels'. He turned the little car over the cattle grid and down the drive. Certainly the place had known better days. The park which now lay on either side of him should have been exquisite. The timber alone was a picture of elms and oaks, though two lay where they had fallen, uprooted in the middle of the grass which grew high and unkempt. The drive ran along the side of the hill before turning slowly to the right and dropping away towards the Manor. From the beginning of this bend Bognor caught his first glimpse of it. It was large, solid and stone and very English. Not a Duke's house. The ancestral home of the Dorsets was, typically, in Norfolk, and this had always been their third or even fourth residence, suitable for cadet branches, younger sons or, as now, eccentric, widowed mothers.

As he drove on it became increasingly clear that the Dorsets had run low on funds. What had once been herbaceous borders were now a mess of weeds and plants gone badly to seed. The lawns were unmown and the house which from a distance had looked so dependable and sturdy was, on closer study, rackety and sad. The mullioned windows, the ugly gremlin gargoyles and the rusting, studded front door were all in need of repair. A line of washing fluttered on what might once, long ago, have been a croquet lawn, and outside the left corner of the house lay a rusting old Austin Seven with no wheels.

Bognor stopped the Mini immediately outside the door and pulled the chain which hung by it. He heard no bell but the instant he rang there was a noise of barking from within. The barking approached and the door was pulled back six inches. A small woman like a wren looked from behind it and said, 'Not today, thank you.'

'I'm not selling anything,' said Bognor, who had met this response before. 'All I want is to ask a few questions.'

'Ah. Hang on a jiffy then.' She shut the door, rattled with the lock and chain, then reopened it releasing a throng of small mustard-coloured dogs which leapt at Bognor's knees.

'Aaagh,' he cried, retreating aghast. One of them grabbed his turn-up in its jaws and started to wrestle with it; another pee-ed on his shoe while the rest jumped and sniffed and jostled him.

'Guy . . . Talisman . . . Waverley . . . Mannering. . . . Down, the lot of you!' shrieked the diminutive Duchess, laying into her dogs with her walking stick. The dogs subsided and the noise dwindled until the entire pack was behind the Duchess's floor-length hearthrug of a skirt and only a single snivel emerged from them. Bognor had never seen a Dandie Dinmont before and they unnerved him. They seemed to him to combine the appearance of a dachshund with that of a poodle and their behaviour reminded him of a hunt terrier that had once belonged to a school friend.

'I'm awfully sorry,' he said, still shocked, 'I'm afraid I'm not terribly good at dogs.'

'So I observe,' said the Duchess drily. 'The absolute A1 cardinal rule is not to let them see that you're afraid of them. They've rumbled you already. Get down, Mannering.' This last remark was directed at a venturesome Dinmont which had surreptitiously launched itself at Bognor's knee from behind. 'Anyway, come along in. No point standing there being eaten alive. I think there may be some gin.'

She ushered Bognor along a dark hallway, in which he was dimly aware of lugubrious country-house portraits by disciples of Lely and Reynolds, and through a door on the left.

'Just a tick,' she said, 'I'll see if we have alcohol.'

Mercifully she took her marauding pack of Dinmonts with her, leaving Bognor to examine his new surroundings. The room reeked of dog. Whereas the Kennel Club and Three Corners had been markedly dogless the Duchess of Dorset's drawing room was a veritable kennel. Dog hairs lay thick on the carpet and chairs, baskets and dog blankets littered the floor, and bowls of water and bowls of biscuit were more frequent than occasional tables. Like Mrs Potts, the Duchess evidently didn't notice the squalor of her immediate surroundings. Everything from the portraits—similar to those in the hall—to the curtains looked filthy. In a corner by the fireplace there was even an old orange box, with 'Outspan Oranges—with care' stencilled on it. Bognor scarcely noticed it on his first glance round the room. Then he did a sudden double take. Could it be? No, this was absurd. Why on earth should Fred, alias Whately Wonderful, be exhumed from his grave in Buckinghamshire and transported to the Duchess of Dorset's drawing room? He stared blankly at the portrait above the mantelpiece, rapt in thought, before suddenly realizing that it was a picture of a dog. It was competently done, if a shade chocolate-boxy. Bognor immediately recognized the distinctive and alarming features of a Dandie Dinmont like the ones that had just assaulted him. He looked down at his shoe and feared that dog's urine would stain. Not that the suedes were new but even so. . . . The expression on the dog's face was one of perky charm. It looked unbearably cute and Bognor, who reckoned he'd got the Dinmont's measure now, found it indescribably flattering. He was about to turn back to the mysterious orange box when he noticed the initials at the bottom of the portrait: 'C.C.' Of course. This was an example of Miss Cordingley's art. It confirmed his impression of dishonesty.

He was about to return to the matter of the orange box when the Dutchess came back with a bottle of Gordon's gin. It was one of those very old bottles with a top with a hinge instead of the newer screw top. 'Not many left now,' she said, brandishing it. 'Almost all the dear dead Duke left me. It killed him, of course, before he could finish it.' She poured out two gins and tonic, handed him one and then stood looking at the picture with him.

'It's by Coriander Cordingley, isn't it?'

'That's right,' she said, 'It's poor Piddlehampton Peter. She's got him to a tee, don't you think? Look at the eyes. You can almost feel the damp on his nose, poor old thing. She's frightfully clever, Coriander. Do you know her?'

'I've met her,' said Bognor. It was on the tip of his tongue to say where he'd met her, but he thought better of it. 'I wouldn't say I really knew her.'

'Not in the Biblical sense, eh?' said the Duchess, kicking one of the dogs towards the sofa. 'I'm most frightfully sorry but I don't think I know your name.'

'Oh,' said Bognor. 'No. I suppose not. How silly. Bognor. Simon Bognor.'

'How nice,' said the Duchess, shaking his hand energetically. 'And I'm Dora Dorset. You don't by any chance breed bassets, do you?'

'No.'

'There's a Bognor near Bournemouth who breeds bassets. I've only seen photographs of him but you are rather alike. Beautiful dogs, too. No relation, I suppose?'

'No.'

'Oh well.' The Duchess looked thoughtfully at her drink. 'I think gin improves with age,' she said. 'Now come and sit down and tell me what I can do for you.' She sat on the sofa and immediately vanished under a pile of dogs. When she'd removed most of them with another display of good-humoured shouting she patted an empty space on her left and motioned to Bognor to join her. He sat down reluctantly.

'Well,' he said, 'I work for a special department at the Board of Trade.'

'How fearfully exciting,' said the Duchess. 'In all my years I don't believe I have ever met an employee of the Board of Trade, least of all from one of their special departments. I'd no idea they had special departments. Do go on.'

Bognor coughed. 'The fact is that I am investigating a matter which could well affect you. Do you know Mervyn Sparks?'

'Horrid little man. Mean mouth and foxy eyes. He was down here the other day on some pretext or other snooping about. I hope he's not a friend of yours.'

'He wasn't,' said Bognor. 'As a matter of fact, he's dead.'

'Is he really?' The Duchess did not seem greatly interested. 'Have you come all the way from London to tell me this? I wouldn't have thought the little man was worth the trouble.'

'I don't think you quite understand, your Grace. The point is, he died of rabies.'

'The silly fellow. I've no doubt he picked it up on one of those damn fool foreign trips of his. You're asking for trouble going to places like that. I haven't been abroad for fifteen years. It's a very over-rated pastime. Do you travel much?'

'Scarcely at all.' Bognor's forensic powers had been thrown into a state of more than usual disarray by the dogs. He was having trouble establishing whether the Duchess was as scatty as she seemed. 'Your Piddlehampton Peter had to be put down because he had rabies, and . . .'

'Ah, Mr Worthing . . .' said the Duchess.

'Bognor.'

'Forgive me, Mr Bognor. Let's not rush our fences. *Suspected* rabies. There has to be a post mortem. Then we shall know. I have my doubts.'

'There is going to be a post mortem?' His gaze strayed inevitably to the orange box, abandoned by the fireplace. The Duchess followed it.

'Of course, Mr Bognor. The dog went quite mad and bit Louise. Naturally the authorities had to be informed. I fear they may have over-reacted, but we shall see.'

'I don't understand how your dog could have contracted rabies, your Grace, but before he died Mr

Sparks told one of our people that he'd been down here and one of your dogs bit him.'

'Did he indeed?' The Duchess seemed for the first time to be disturbed. She took a deeper than usual draught of gin. 'Perhaps. Yes. I do recall the incident. He tried to pick someone up. Ridiculous. The man has . . . had . . . no sense whatever. Lunacy to allow him out in a show ring. Naturally the dog bit him, but it was no more than a nip. A tiny bite. Hardly worth talking about.'

'In this case,' said Bognor, profoundly, 'a nip is as good as a feast.'

She looked at him sharply. 'What a very odd thing to say,' she said. 'Are you suggesting that Mr Sparks died because he was bitten by one of my dogs?'

'Um.' Bognor thought for a moment. 'Yes,' he said eventually, 'I think I am.'

'Oh.' They sat in silence only punctuated by the playful snorts and whimpers of the dogs.

'Is Miss Cordingley staying with you?' he asked abruptly.

The Duchess seemed taken aback. 'Coriander? Good heavens, no. She usually stays at the Dorset Arms in the village.'

'Usually?'

'It takes time to prepare a portrait,' she said. 'There have to be a great many sittings.'

'Even for a dog?'

The Duchess, who had gone over to refill their glasses, drew herself up to her full height, which Bognor estimated at no more than five feet.

'I am not referring to dogs, Mr Bognor,' she said, grandly. 'I am talking about myself.'

'I don't understand.'

'Coriander is painting a portrait of me.'

'I thought she only painted dogs.'

'There is no need to be impertinent, young man.'

Bognor blushed. 'I wasn't. I meant I honestly didn't . . .'

The Duchess returned to the sofa with their drinks.

Bognor continued: 'Is she with you today?' He could think of no other way of explaining the Outspan box.

The Duchess shook her head. 'Not possible; I am expecting her, of course. We have a sitting arranged for tomorrow morning, and I expect her for dinner tonight.' A thought appeared to come to her unexpectedly. 'Perhaps you'd care to dine? Though I hardly think . . .' She degenerated into a mutter but Bognor thought he heard her say something about there being no accounting for taste.

'I'm sorry,' he said, 'but I have to get back to London.'

Even as he said it he realized that he couldn't return to London without establishing the contents of the orange box. He hesitated.

'It's late to be driving all that way,' said the Duchess. 'I really think you'd do better to stay. The Dorset Arms are bound to have a room.'

'Well, perhaps . . .'

The Duchess clapped her hands in an anachronistically girlish gesture.

'That's settled then. You'll have to take pot luck, I'm afraid. I'm staffless now that even poor Louise has gone home to her mother, but I shall be able to rustle something up.' She looked at her watch. 'It's late already. Shall we say half-past seven for eight? And there's no need to dress. We're very informal in the country.'

Bognor accepted as gracefully as he could manage. The dogs were still worrying him, but he realized that duty called; and at least he didn't have to spend the night in this derelict old house. On the way out he noticed that the damp in the hall was so bad that it stood out in beads of moisture like condensation on a champagne bottle.

3

The Dorset Arms was as much of a caricature as the rest of the village. A long, low, pink building with a hat of thatch, its air of implausibility was strengthened by the fact that it advertised American Express and Diners Club in its window. Outside on the forecourt a white Morgan sports car was parked and when Bognor signed the register he noticed that the name above his own was 'Ms C. Cordingley' of Bicester Mews, W.11. He had been right.

The hotel had obviously been taken over by an enterprising and wealthy management in the recent past for Bognor's room had its own bath and telephone —not the luxuries he normally associated with country pubs. He had half an hour before his appointment at the manor and he would have to tell Monica that he wasn't coming home. Better not tell her he was sharing a hotel with Coriander Cordingley.

'Oh, hell,' she said, 'I wanted to go out this evening. I felt like a curry.'

'Well, go and have a curry.'

'I might. I'll get Hugo to take me.' She sounded petulant. Hugo was a constant unsuccessful suitor, who despite five years of hot pursuit had continued to try. Both Bognor and Monica had decided long ago that it was her unattainability which made her so attractive to him. If she'd accepted one of his clumsy advances he would have been scared rigid.

'Any messages?'

'The office just rang. They said to hurry with the cake tin, whatever that means, and a man called Watherspoon rang from the Kennel Club. Apparently he's got what you wanted.'

'Has he just?' Bognor hoped it would help him. 'Did he leave a home number?'

'Yes. It's a Reigate one. Hang on . . .' He scribbled the number down and thanked her. 'Don't mention it,' she said.

'I'm sorry I've got to stay the night,' he said. 'It's not my idea of fun.'

'Nor mine,' she said, curtly. Then she relented. 'You will be all right, won't you?'

'I'll try. Must go now. See you tomorrow.'

'O.K.'

He sat on the end of the bed and hoped she'd go out for the curry. It would make him feel less guilty, though why he should feel guilty he couldn't think. The call to Reigate took a long time, but eventually the operator rang from downstairs and put him through. A woman's voice answered and he asked to speak to the voice's husband. Almost immediately Watherspoon came on.

'Most extraordinary,' he said. He sounded very excited. 'I've found two in the last three weeks.'

'Two what?'

'Dandie Dinmonts. One at the Great Mid-Western Dog Show in Cairo, Illinois, and the other at the Club Canino Colombiano's Show in Bogota. Best of Show in both cases. The Great Mid-Western was exactly two weeks ago and Bogota was five days before that.'

Bognor whistled down the receiver.

'Sorry,' said Watherspoon. 'What?'

'Nothing. I just whistled. I'm amazed.'

'So was I. No one here has ever heard of a Dinmont doing anything outside Britain. They're not popular abroad.'

'I can imagine,' said Bognor. 'Two different dogs? There'd be plenty of time to get from Bogota to Cairo.'

'Same dog. Well, same name. Rob Roy of Lost Horizons. The owner is Edgar J. Eagerly.'

'Eagerly?'

'Yes,' said Watherspoon. 'Have you come across him?'

'I may have done,' said Bognor, mind beginning to race. 'I'm not sure.'

'He's very well known in the States. Highly eccentric. His father made a fortune out of soda fountains in the thirties and Edgar J. has this incredible place in the Appalachians called the Dog Centre. Have you heard of that?'

'No.'

'He does everything there. All sorts of research projects on dogs. Genetics, nutrition, psychology. You name it; but I'd never heard of him showing anywhere. Let alone Dandie Dinmonts. Most of his work is consultancy.'

'Funny.'

'That's not the only thing which is a bit funny. Both those shows had the same judge for Best of Show *and* for terrier class, which is what the Dinmont would have to have won to be nominated for Best of Show. And that was Percy Pocklington.'

'I've heard of him too.' Watherspoon had paused for effect. Obviously a great many people had heard of Percy Pocklington. 'What's he like?'

Watherspoon lowered his voice. 'I shouldn't say this really and I wouldn't if I were in the office but between you and me he's an absolute scheister. He's the man who started the Dog-lovers' League. It gets little old ladies to leave it money, does no good for anyone, least of all dogs, and pays what Percy likes to call "an honorarium". Some honorarium. I believe it's almost ten thousand a year.'

Bognor grunted and looked at his watch.

'I must go now, Mr Watherspoon. You've been enormously helpful. I can't tell you how grateful I am. I expect to be in touch again. Goodbye.'

He would have to hurry. Only ten minutes before dinner at the Duchess's. No time even for a quick shave. Instead he put a handkerchief in his breast pocket, dabbed on some Old Spice Burley and hurried downstairs. Outside he noticed that the white Morgan had vanished. That meant he would be the last to arrive. He drove up the village street at fifty, crashing the gears in his excitement, and wondering if he'd been over-lavish with the aftershave.

The dusk was almost turning to darkness as he arrived at the house. Not only was Miss Cordingley there already, she was standing at the corner of what had once been a flowerbed, watching as the tiny Duchess of Dorset did some digging. By the time he'd parked they had finished the gardening and were walking towards him. The Duchess was at least six inches shorter than Coriander and was having to take twice as many steps to keep up.

Bognor went to meet them.

'Good evening,' said the Duchess, still wearing the hearthrug she'd worn earlier. The spade was over her shoulder. 'Sometimes I attempt to revitalize the garden, but as you can see it's too much for an old woman and it's absolutely impossible to get help these days. You two have met, I believe.'

He and Coriander shook hands. Again she held his hand gently and a little long. She also looked straight at him as she did. Bognor found this disconcerting and allowed his own eyes to drift downwards to the breastline. With a gratifying shock of pleasure he realized that the portraitist was wearing a diaphanous blouse with no bra underneath. He wondered if she'd known he was coming to dinner.

'How amusing to find you here of all places,' she said. 'Have you made any progress?'

'I think perhaps I have,' he said. 'It's too early to be quite certain.'

The Duchess shivered slightly. 'Getting cold,' she said, 'and the midges are biting. Let's see if there's some of that gin left.' Since she'd opened the bottle little more than half an hour before, Bognor very much hoped there would be. There was.

It was dark in the drawing room and the Duchess had only had one light on—a low wattage standard lamp in a corner which did little more than cast shadows. The dogs, who had obviously not been allowed to share in the gardening, welcomed them noisily, and in the gloaming Bognor managed a satisfying little kick which caught one of them in the chest. It let out a yelp and both women looked at him suspiciously. Coriander gave the ghost of a smile. Despite the lack of light Bognor was able to see that where the orange box had been there was now nothing.

After she'd dispensed three stiff gins the Duchess departed 'to see what I can rustle up', declining all offers of help in the kitchen.

'I think I ought to warn you,' said Coriander when she'd left, taking the dogs with her, 'the food here is ghastly. I don't believe Dora has any taste buds at all; and as you've probably gathered she doesn't have much cash either.'

'I thought she made a success of her dogs.'

'As far as it's possible, yes. But there isn't a great deal to be made from Dandies. Virtually no export demand. In any case it must cost a fortune to keep this place up.'

'But she doesn't anyway.'

Miss Cordingley had been standing by the windows, a slender silhouette in a long clinging skirt.

'That's unfair,' she said. 'You're at the Dorset Arms, I hear?'

'Yes. So are you.'

'Mmmm,' she said, suggesting all while saying nothing. She came and sat next to him on the sofa, where her scent eliminated all traces of dog smell as well as overpowering Bognor's aftershave.

'We could have a drink at the Dorset after dinner,' he said, conscious that she had sat a great deal nearer to him than was absolutely necessary.

'Mmmm,' she said again. 'It might wash away the taste.'

She laughed a throaty, gurgly little giggle and Bognor,

pleasantly warmed with gin, began to relax. Perhaps the evening would be better than he'd feared. Then he suddenly felt a twinge of pain in his arm. It also seemed to have become very hot.

'Is it hot in here?' he asked.

'Don't be ridiculous,' she laughed again, but Bognor was no longer in the mood to be lulled by her sensuality. 'It's perishing. Dora hasn't had any heat in this house for years.'

'I feel hot,' he said.

'Let's feel,' she said, and put a hand on his forehead. He felt rotten.

After holding her hand there for a few moments she said 'Mmmm' again. 'You *are* hot,' she said, 'you feel ill.'

'You're right, I do feel ill,' he said, then he remembered the early morning. He had never suffered reactions to his typhoid injections, but never before had he so far forgotten himself as to drink gin afterwards. 'Hell,' he said with a vehemence which made Coriander start.

'What?' she asked.

'Anti-typhoid jab,' he said, 'I had one this morning. It's beginning to play up.'

'Oh, poor man. It will. You're not supposed to drink alcohol. Absolute unadulterated hell.'

'So everyone tells me.' He winced as another stab of pain lacerated his stomach. 'I don't somehow think,' he went on, 'that you are a bringer of good fortune. You always seem to turn up when there's death and destruction around.'

'You could say the same about you. You're pretty much an angel of death yourself.'

'It's my job.' The pain was getting worse every second.

'Ah.'

He decided to be more conciliatory. He had a firm impression that Miss Cordingley was a constant factor in this investigation.

'I didn't know you did human portraits,' he said.

'I prefer it,' she said, perceptibly relaxing. 'After all, I was at the Slade. Unfortunately it's difficult to get established. You really need money to do it successfully. That's why I do the dogs.'

'How far have you got with Dora?'

'I've got my sketches back at the hotel. I'll show them to you after dinner if you like.'

Half an hour earlier the invitation would have been irresistible. Now the pains were sweeping over him with growing regularity. It was like being raked with machine-gun fire and he could feel the sweat running down his nose. He dabbed at it with a handkerchief.

As he did so the Duchess returned.

'Grub up,' she said. 'Surprising what you can find when you have to. Some of the tins looked a bit rusty but it was all on the outside.'

Coriander squeezed his thigh lightly. 'Courage,' she said softly, pronouncing it the French way with the last syllable accentuated as in camouflage. Bognor felt too ill to react.

The Duchess, chattering brightly about the longevity of tinned foods, now conducted them down more corridors, heavy with oil paintings and bits of armour, cumbersome chests, almost completely devoid of light. There were no carpets and their footsteps echoed eerily. He bet the doctor had used a rusty needle.

After a long march stumbling after the dogs, they emerged into candlelight. This came from two heavy silver candlesticks, much tarnished with neglect, which stood at either end of an oak table designed to seat about sixty in comfort.

'I've put us all up one end,' said the Duchess. 'When Dickie was alive and we were at the castle we used to sit at opposite ends of a table even bigger than this— just the two of us. I always said we ought to have walkie-talkie sets, but Dickie said the servants wouldn't like it. So that was that. Half a mo' and I'll get the soup.'

She bustled off. Bognor shivered, suddenly frozen with cold. It was as if the machine-gunners who had been strafing his stomach had substituted icicles for bullets.

'You can't really see it in the dark,' said Coriander, 'but there's the most marvellous stained glass. This used to be the chapel.'

Bognor looked blankly at the darkened windows and on up to the vaulted ceiling. 'The Dorsets always stayed Catholic,' continued Coriander. 'They used to say Mass here all through Queen Elizabeth's reign. And Cromwell. Jolly brave.'

'Jolly,' said Bognor. There was a bottle on the table, in a Georgian coaster. He picked it up to examine the label. 'Good God,' he said, 'Lafite '61.'

'That's good, isn't it?' said the Duchess who'd come back with the soup. 'I'm a champagne girl myself but I remember Dickie ordering that. It arrived after he died. Sad.'

She brought the tray up to their end of the table and handed out the three bowls, which were elaborate two-handled blue and white china, chased with gold. Bognor had no idea what it was but it felt expensive. The soup spoons were silver with the Dorset dragon on the handle.

'Mr Bognor,' said the Duchess, 'perhaps you'd taste the wine.'

He thought for a moment, then decided that having taken gin already Lafite could scarcely make him worse. He poured some into his crystal goblet and drank. Even with his artificially induced pains he could appreciate it.

'Marvellous,' he said, and poured it out. Then he tried the soup. It was tepid tinned tomato.

'What is your christian name, Mr Bognor?' the Duchess was asking.

He told her.

'Well then, Simon, now we're all sitting comfortable, do please tell us exactly what it is that you suspect?'

He told them as briefly as he could, saying nothing about Mrs Potts' missing orange box or the astounding success of Dandie Dinmonts in Bogota and Cairo, Illinois.

When he'd done, the Duchess clapped her hands. 'How exciting,' she said, 'and Mr Sparks is dead which makes it even more mysterious. I suppose he was the man who was really on to it.'

'Sparks dead?' said Coriander sharply. 'Nobody told me that. When did it happen? Why didn't you tell me, Dora?'

'I quite forgot,' said the Duchess placidly. She collected the soup bowls and left them again.

'Was he a friend of yours then?' asked Bognor.

'I thought he was a horrid little man,' she said, 'I knew him a bit. He certainly wasn't a friend. He once made a pass at me in Warsaw when I was painting Mr Gomulka's bloodhound. He was judging the local show. What did he die of?'

'Rabies.'

Miss Cordingley looked at him very hard.

'Honestly?' she asked after a bit.

'Yes, honestly.'

'Christ,' she said.

The next course was corned beef, processed peas and tinned boiled potatoes.

'I thought of turning the beef into hash or fritters,' said the Duchess, 'but I don't think I could. I used to do it in the war when I was in the ATS.'

'It's very nice as it is,' said Coriander loyally.

'Fray Bentos,' said the Duchess. 'Dickie bought a job lot when there was an atom bomb scare. I think it may have been something to do with the Berlin airlift.'

Bognor didn't enjoy it. They talked about the dog world and he tried to acquire general knowledge without appearing to pry into the particular. He did ask about Edgar J. Eagerly and Percy Pocklington but got no very useful information about either. He had a distinct impression that both women were being deliberately non-committal.

'Now,' said the Duchess when they'd fought their

way through the main course. 'Tinned peaches or fresh oranges?'

All opted for oranges and they were brought in, in a delicate silver fruit basket. Bognor's orange had 'Outspan' stamped on it. It jogged his memory which had been flagging under the physical assault of his injection and the gastronomic assault of dinner.

'Outspan,' he said very deliberately. 'Do you buy in bulk, your Grace?'

'What an extraordinary question. Why do you ask?'

'Just idle curiosity,' he said. This time he was aware that he had alerted them both. He was almost certain now that the Duchess had been burying the orange box when he arrived for dinner and fairly certain that the orange box contained the remains of Fred. He wondered what the cake tin in his boot contained.

'We're having a post mortem done on Ailsa Potts' dead dog,' he said, trying to provoke a response. 'It'll be interesting to see what it shows.' Nothing happened. Both women muttered a neutral 'yes', but it was said with self-satisfaction. He was convinced now, but he still couldn't understand why they should go to such lengths to protect Mrs Potts. If the dog could be proved to have had rabies that would be Mrs Potts' problem, unless, of course, they were afraid she'd give away the secrets of the smuggling network. Always assuming . . . he groaned inwardly. It would be easier to make a list. As soon as things began to get complicated he liked to unravel them on paper. Otherwise they invariably stayed ravelled. He was not by nature methodical.

'Coffee?' asked the Duchess.

It was lukewarm when it arrived but Dora announced that there was good brandy in the drawing room and they retraced their steps. This time the Duchess took one of the candlesticks and guided them with it. It was a feeble guttering light but enough to see by.

'Are you feeling awful?' whispered Coriander.

'Yes.'

'Never mind. We can go soon. I'll show you those sketches of Dora.'

Normally he'd have been delighted. Such obvious sexual advances seldom came his way. With a slight sense of remorse he wondered if Monica had gone out for the curry.

The brandy was good. He swilled it round his mouth and hoped it would prove medicinal. His pains were appalling. They encouraged him to make further mischief.

'I hear,' he said, 'that Dandie Dinmonts are beginning to take off abroad.'

'Oh?' The Duchess was a little too innocent. 'I've heard no such thing.'

'I understand a Dandie Dinmont was Best of Show in Bogota and at the Great Mid-Western.'

'Really,' said the Duchess. 'I'm afraid *Our Dogs* has very little foreign news. Besides the print is too small. I simply can't read it.'

'You're very well informed,' said Coriander. She sounded distinctly frigid. 'I thought you didn't know anything about dogs.'

'I didn't,' he said, 'but I'm finding out.'

He braced himself. He didn't feel up to a row but he couldn't leave without having made some effort.

'Look,' he said, 'I don't want to seem boorish, your Grace, but the Kennel Club were very surprised indeed that Dandie Dinmonts had won those two shows. And your dog is suspected of having died of rabies. Isn't it just possible that it was your own dog that actually won two prizes?'

'Oh really.' The Duchess was obviously angry, though he wasn't sure whether or not it was contrived.

'I've already told you,' she continued, 'I haven't left the country for years. I can show you my passport.'

'They don't stamp passports these days.'

'You need a visa for America and I don't have one. What is more my passport's expired.'

'That's all very well but I wasn't suggesting that you won the prizes. I think your dog may have been in Cairo and Bogota but I don't suppose you were for a minute. That would give the whole thing away—not,'

he added hastily, 'that I'm suggesting you were involved. Much more likely that the dog was kidnapped.
The man who showed it was Edgar J. Eagerly, so I
should imagine your presence would be entirely superfluous.'

'You really have done a lot of homework.' It was
Coriander. Her voice was light and patronizing. 'But to
an objective outsider the idea does seem rather pre-
posterous.'

'Who said anything about your being an objective
outsider?'

The pains in his stomach were making him almost
too aggressive. He recognized it and tried to calm himself.

'What I mean is that you have shown a peculiar
facility for cropping up in places where I am taken by
suspicion. What's more,' he felt himself become in-
discreet but was unable to stop, 'I believe that you and
Ailsa Potts dug that dog up after I'd seen you burying
it, and that you brought it down here in its orange box
to prevent our conducting a post mortem on it.'

'If that's what happened, what are you having your
post mortem done on at the moment?' she asked. 'You
said you were having one done. What did you exhume?'

'God knows,' said Bognor, 'but I'm jolly sure it
wasn't Fred.'

'All right then, if you're right and for some reason
best known to you I dug up the corpse and brought it
down to Dora's, where is it now?'

He had to admire her poise. The only indication that
she might be losing her cool were her nipples which
were heaving quite alarmingly under her chiffon blouse.

'Outside in the flowerbed where you buried it before
dinner,' he said, grimly aware, despite his throbbing
arm and stomach, that he was sounding like some Victorian parlour game.

'All right then, go and get it,' said Coriander, now
allowing herself to appear irritated.

'Children, children,' shouted the Duchess, so loudly
that the dogs began to bark. 'This is most unseemly.

May I suggest, with the wisdom of years that we sleep on the matter before it becomes any more ridiculous and acrimonious.'

Simon and Coriander glowered at each other. The Duchess poured out more brandy. They still glowered. Then Coriander broke into a ravishing smile.

'Dora's quite right,' she said. 'Let's be friends. So much more attractive. Anyway, I am tired. I think I am going back to the Dorset Arms.'

She drained her brandy with a flourish and Bognor did the same, though without the flourish. The Duchess looked relieved. Bognor felt defeated.

Back at the hotel, which he and Coriander reached in convoy, they entered together.

'Are we going to have that drink?' she asked, in the hall.

'Honestly,' he said, 'normally I'd like nothing better, but I really do feel bloody.' That was true. 'And,' he continued, 'I'm going to go straight to bed.' That was not true.

To his surprise she kissed him. Quite lightly but with a definite suggestion that, should he wish, there might be more to follow.

'Good night then,' she said. 'Some other time perhaps. I have a feeling we may see more of each other over the next few weeks.'

Unfortunately he had more work to do. He knew that if he stuck to his promise and insisted on searching for the orange box next morning, then it would not be there. His only chance of finding it was to go back to the Manor now. It was not a happy prospect, but over his years with the Board of Trade he had acquired a stern, unbending sense of duty.

Upstairs he lay on the bed and waited. He daren't go to sleep for fear of not waking till next morning. Anyway he doubted whether he would have slept. The pain would have kept him awake. Because he hadn't expected to stay the night he had no toothbrush, toothpaste, pyjamas, let alone the aspirin which he badly wanted.

Nor a book to read. He groaned. It was only just after ten. Luckily the country went to bed early and if he waited an hour he might be able to go to the Duchess's in safety. It would be best, in the circumstances, if he drove straight back to London after he'd excavated the orange box. The morning could be embarrassing.

After five minutes staring at the ceiling and alternating between extremes of heat and cold he decided to have a bath. There was new soap and also Badedas. The luxury impressed him and he wondered if there might be some sort of room service. He turned on the hot tap and went to the phone. To his surprise it answered at once and a friendly Dorset burr promised to bring a bottle of aspirins at once. The voice was as good as its word and the drugs appeared in a couple of minutes. He took four.

The bath was as therapeutic as the aspirins. Too therapeutic. When he woke it was because he was cold and damp and he realized with a shock that he had dozed off under the combined influence of the aspirin and the hot water. Now the water was almost cold and he'd lost the benefit of the exercise. His watch showed that it was half-past eleven, which was a reasonable time for setting out on his expedition. He dressed slowly and swallowed two more aspirins, then went to the window and looked out over the village. There was a full moon which enabled him to see the outline of every house in the place, but there wasn't an artificial light visible, nor a person. Opening the casement he strained to hear any sound of nocturnal life but there was nothing, not even an owl. He gave a half smile of satisfaction. It was about the first thing that had gone right so far. He wondered if Monica was asleep or if she was worrying about him. Perhaps she'd forgotten him. He was glad she didn't know what he was up to.

The hotel was quiet as he crept downstairs in stockinged feet, his suedes held tightly in his left hand. He hoped no night porter would appear since the obvious inference to be drawn was that he was a penniless

guest doing a moonlight flit. They'd probably accuse
him of stealing an ashtray or some soap.

The car started first time. It had been parked alongside Coriander's white Morgan and he was relieved to
see that that was still there. That young lady, he hoped,
was safely tucked up in bed and fast asleep. For an
instant he thought wistfully that he might, under slightly
different circumstances, have been tucked up with her,
but a stab of pain in his arm reminded him of his duty.
The moon was absurdly bright and it was quite safe to
drive without lights. He did so and kept the car at
fifteen miles an hour in second gear. At the disused
lodge he pulled over on to the grass and turned off the
engine. It would be safer to continue on foot.

There was a torch in the car but it was so light that
he decided to leave it. He had no spade or other im-
plement so, he realized glumly, he would either have to
scrabble with his bare hands or find something in an
outhouse. Probably bare hands, which would be tiresome, but he doubted whether the orange box would
be far below the soil's surface. He set off, walking down
the middle of the drive. He was out of sight of the
house and there was no need for undue caution until
he reached the bend in the road. At that point he could
take to the parkland. The grass was so high that if he
crouched he would be invisible. The thought of cover-
ing the final three hundred yards at the crouch did not
appeal but it was inevitable.

It was still amazingly quiet. His feet on the remains of
the gravel made a noise like a regiment of light infantry
and he crossed to the grass at the side of the road near
the railings. The air was rich with the smell of animal
excrement and wild flowers. He inhaled happily. It was
warm too. A little further he half stumbled in a hole,
swore in a loud whisper, and startled a sheep which
had been asleep a few yards away. It baa-ed an objec-
tion, then subsided again. Bognor froze for a minute
and then walked on, more cautiously now. From the
direction of the village he heard a car. Some late night
reveller returning from a country frolic, no doubt. Or

an illicit lover wending his way homewards after a
tragic tryst. This was Thomas Hardy country. The engine sounded raw like a racing car. Then just as it
reached the end of the drive it slowed to a dull purr
for a moment. Bognor frowned and paused. Why had
it stopped?

Just as he turned to watch, he heard the engine roar
and the tyres squeal as the machine spun to its right
and began to hurtle down the drive. A second later
and he would have been caught in the headlights like
a trapped rabbit. Instead with lightning reflexes which
subsequently amazed him and became a matter for
massive self-congratulation he leapt the railings and
flattened himself in the long grass. Seconds later the
car shrieked past, took the bend ahead on two wheels,
steadied itself and bombed on towards the house. He
lay still, listening to the retreating vehicle, heard it skid
to a stop, and only when the engine had been turned
off and the doors slammed did he get to his feet cursing
noisily. His stomach felt damp and the smell of dung,
which had previously been a pleasantly rural suggestion, was now a painfully overstated fact. He had dived
into a cowpat.

Now he hurried. The moon had shown him that the
car was a white sports car and he knew what that
meant. Miss Cordingley must have been disturbed by
his departure, investigated it and found the Mini missing. She would rightly assume that he had come for
the body and her assumptions would have been confirmed by the discovery of his car at the end of the
drive. Now she would wake up the Duchess and the two
of them would once more unbury the corpse and remove it to another hiding place. He started to run
through the parkland, keeping his head well down. Before long he came to an oak and he stood upright and
peered round it. He was now only a hundred and fifty
yards from the house which was illuminated by the
moon so that it seemed almost fluorescent, drained of
colour, like the haunted mansion in a very old black
and white movie. In front of it he saw the little white

Morgan and also, to his surprise and alarm, another car—a nondescript square biscuit tin of the sort that firms issue to their commercial travellers.

He continued his advance, still grimly aware of the damp stinking patch on his shirt front and the continuing pain of his injection. He had got to within twenty yards of Fred's flowerbed when the front door opened and three figures emerged. He could only see shapes, but the Duchess and Coriander were easily distinguished if only because of the disparity in their size. The Dandie Dinmonts cavorted at their feet and Bognor swore miserably. The bloody animals would be sure to sniff him out. He remained in a frozen uncomfortable crouch and tried to work out who the third person could be. It was a male figure taller than either of the women and it looked self-possessed. It had one hand in a pocket and the other clasped round a cigarette which glowed bright in the night air. He couldn't hear what was being said but he could see that Coriander was explaining. Her shoulders heaved up and down and her hands waved to emphasize the force of whatever argument she was propounding. She obviously won it because the man shrugged and turned. The three of them began to walk towards the flowerbed. The two women strode purposefully, the man strolled casually—almost languidly. They stopped at the spot which, Bognor judged, marked Fred's most recent grave and the man scuffed at the earth with the toe of his shoe. Now Bognor could just make out what was being said.

'He hasn't got here yet then,' said the man. 'My guess is he'll have turned tail and scuttled for home by now, if he's as wet as you both say. He'll have been warned off by Coriander's flying entrance.'

Bognor winced and held his breath.

'I'm not sure he's as wet as he seems,' said Coriander. Bognor wondered if that was a compliment. 'I don't think we should take the risk. I vote we dig the box up again and you can take it away.'

'I think the girl's right,' said the Duchess. 'No point taking any undue risks.'

The man flicked the stub of his cigarette in Bognor's direction. It landed about ten yards short of his position.

'We'll compromise,' said the man. 'One more glass of Dora's exquisite cognac and then, thus fortified, I will perform the exhumation myself.'

He spoke in an oddly affected way with a drawl and an Oxford accent which were both a little too good to be true. Bognor guessed he had had to work hard at them.

'Oh, all right,' said Coriander, 'one quick glass.'

They turned to walk back to the house accompanied by the dogs who, mercifully, had not noticed him. Bognor watched the front door slam and gulped. He guessed that if he crouched behind the shrubs in the border he might just be able to perform his excavations without being seen from the house—even supposing that they bothered to look out. Which he doubted. They seemed very sure of themselves.

Getting the box back to the car was going to be a problem too, but he would have to face that when he came to it. The instant the door shut he ran to the flowerbed and knelt behind an azalea. It was easy to see even by moonlight where the digging had been done. It was the only earth which had been overturned for years. Everywhere else was solid with flowers and weeds. Immediately he started to scrabble at the ground with his fingers. It was not as hard as he'd feared. The soil was still loosely packed where the Duchess had thrown it back earlier in the day. Within minutes his efforts were rewarded and he felt something solid. He scraped away and managed to distinguish the hard lines of a corner. A little more scraping and he had uncovered the whole of the top of the box. The sweat was pouring down his face now for, injection apart, he had been working much harder than he realized. He paused for breath and looked over towards the Manor. The door was still shut, the light was still on and the curtains were thin. Through them he could just discern shapes. It looked good. With any luck they'd have a second glass. He went back to his work. After a little more scraping he managed to get some purchase on one of the corners, but heave as he might the box remained firmly lodged. He would have to remove more earth. After a few more handfuls he tried again. The box moved a little but it was still wedged too tight. He rocked it to and fro but still it wouldn't come and he returned to his digging. His fingers ached now, adding to his other discomforts. The aspirin was wearing off and the hot and cold machine-gunning was becoming more persistent. The cowpat on his front was beginning to congeal, caking his skin and amalgamating with the rivulets of perspiration. He found some relief in swearing to himself, and dug ever more furiously. At the next attempt the box moved much more. With a final effort he gave a heave and to his pleasure it came away from the enveloping earth. He fell back into the shrubbery making a crash which he was sure would be heard all over Dorset.

Even as he fell he saw the front door open, and the Duchess and the animal portraitist emerged into the moonlight. Once more, however, luck seemed to favour him. Without his noticing, clouds had started to bank up. A small one hid the moon fleetingly, just as the two women were half-way towards him. He heard them talking, and discerned the word 'torch', then footsteps returned to the house. The door slammed. He had a respite and for a moment the darkness was total. He picked up the orange box. It was heavier than he'd hoped, and bigger, but he could just manage. He would have to stop every few minutes anyway. It would not be safe to run in the full glare of the moon. He just managed to complete his first clumsy dash of twenty yards when he heard the door slam. Craning through the grass he saw that the two women now had their torch. Luckily it was only a pocket torch. Bright enough to dig by but not to conduct a chase by. As he lay panting with exhaustion the moon came out from the cloud. He swore once more but saw that the clouds were swelling now and moving fast towards the light. Another thirty seconds, he judged, and it would be safe to run. He prayed that the women would not have discovered the missing crate by then. They didn't, and as darkness descended he scampered off clutching his trophy to his dung-sodden chest, optimism finally beginning to raise his spirits.

Whether it was the aspirin or the injection or pure over-confidence he never knew, but whatever caused it the result was idiocy. He was still in full pelt when the moon came out again. For an instant he was clearly visible and when he sank to the ground it was with a distinctly audible thud and gasp that could have been heard all over the grounds. But worse, much worse, he had forgotten the third person. Only the women were behind him. The man had obviously been to fetch the spade and had, unknown to Bognor, used a back entrance. Just as the moon lit the park, just as he crashed to earth, he realized that the man was standing barely a yard in front of him. He didn't have a hope. Exhausted and prone on his orange box he only had time to jerk his head upwards and see the karate chop descending towards him. Unconsciousness followed with merciful speed. There was scarcely time for more pain.

4

'Perhaps, dear Simon, that will teach you that alcohol may turn on your desire, but it does precious little for your performance. Didn't you read *Macbeth* at school?'

Coriander Cordingley sat on the end of the bed and smiled at him. She was wearing a white shirt and purple slacks. To his surprise Bognor realized that underneath the blankets he was wearing nothing at all.

'What on earth?' he asked. 'What on earth are you doing here?'

'*Me?*' asked Miss Cordingley giggling, 'what am *I* doing here? That, if you'll pardon the expression, is a bit rich. This just happens to be my room if you remember. I belong here. The correct question is, "What on earth are *you* doing here?"'

'Oh God.' Bognor's aches and pains were returning now. He groaned.

'If you're feeling ill,' she said, 'you have only yourself to blame. Alcohol and anti-typhoid injections and aspirin as well according to the hall porter. No wonder you passed out.'

'Me, passed out?'

Bognor felt his head. There was no bump. The back of his neck was sore, but not as sore as his stomach.

'What are you talking about?'

She smiled at him, infinitely patronizing, oozing mock pity.

'You really don't remember?'

Bognor's memory was still incomplete but he definitely recalled his drive to Piddlehampton Manor, his discovery of the orange box. More came flooding back as he tried desperately to remember it. Particularly the final act. The tall dark stranger with the pseudo-effete voice, administering the *coup de grâce*. However, his faculties were returning.

'Remember anything? Me? No, not a thing?'

Coriander gave a smirk of satisfaction.

'Brace yourself,' she said. 'It may come as rather a shock. Perhaps you didn't realize you were such a potential Lothario. Still, *in aspirin veritas*. Or aspirin, *vino* and typhoid and cholera serum. . . . You remember coming back from Dora's?'

'Yes.'

'And you'd had gin, claret and one too many brandies.'

'I disagree about one too many.'

'Maybe not usually, but you had had that jab. Then you made it worse with the aspirin and I rather suspect you had a bottle in your room, but I won't press that suggestion.'

She was purring like a Siamese. Bognor suddenly began to find her story dreadfully plausible.

'Well,' she continued, 'I'd just got undressed when you knocked at the door with an absurd suggestion about my showing you the sketches I'd done of Dora. I knew that wasn't what you'd come for, and you knew I knew that wasn't what you'd come for, and as a matter of fact it was all shaping up for a very happy night together when I suddenly realized you were as pissed as a newt, and no sooner had you got into the room and taken your clothes off than you were out like a light.'

She pouted with humorous petulance. 'Not very flattering for a girl,' she said. 'I hope you don't make a habit of it.'

Bognor lay back and frowned. He would have to think about it.

'Are you sure?' he asked.

'Straight out. You didn't even kiss me.'

'That's not what I meant.'

She smiled again. 'You really don't remember?'

'No.'

'Well, I promise you it's absolute gospel.' She stood up and became brisk.

'Now I have to get back to London. I do hope we meet again soon. You've got my number and I think after your performance last night you definitely owe me something, even if it's only a drink.'

She walked over to the pillow and kissed him. 'You still don't look very well,' she said. 'If I were you I'd go back to sleep. Bye-bye.'

She picked up a slim leather suitcase, gave him an airy wave and was gone.

Bognor sat up and then, because the effort made him feel sick, lay down again.

'What an absurd story,' he said out loud. The time had come, he knew, to make a comprehensive list of all that had happened. Otherwise he was going to be hopelessly duped. He knew that after the strange man had slugged him they must have brought him back and dumped him in Coriander's bed, but how could he possibly prove this version to anybody else? It was hard enough to convince himself.

He was in London again before lunch. A heavy mixed grill of a breakfast and the clear blue of a perfect summer sky put him in a better mood and his staggering lack of success made him positively light-headed. The stomach pains had disappeared and to his puzzlement there was still no bruising or even pain where he had been hit during the night. His attacker must have felled him with a professionally placed and executed blow to have left him unblemished. That in itself was unnerving. He had assumed that he was up against amateurs. The thought that one of the dog smugglers was an expert in unarmed combat made him distinctly depressed.

So too did the prospect of Parkinson and when, after making arrangements for the cake tin to be dealt with, he found himself in the sparsely furnished office of his superior, the reality proved as unpleasant as his fore-bodings.

He gave a slightly bowdlerized account of the pre-vious twenty-four hours, keeping his eyes fixed firmly on the portrait of Her Majesty the Queen which hung above Parkinson's head.

'Would you recognize the man again?' asked Par-kinson, his expression hovering between incredulity and great weariness.

'I'd know his voice.'

'Hmmm.' Parkinson's fingers drummed sharply on his blotter.

'Surely to God you could have done better than this?' he asked, the same mixture of irritation and hopelessness fighting in his voice.

Bognor moved his gaze from the monarch to the lino at his feet. He thought of trying to reply and then de-cided that the question was rhetorical. After another unhealthy pause Parkinson spoke again.

'What are your suspicions then?' he asked, managing to suggest that although he was bound to listen to them, he asked only as a polite formality.

'It seems,' said Bognor, picking his words very deliberately, 'to me, that the Dandie Dinmont in Co-lombia and America was almost certainly the Duchess's and that Sparks contracted rabies after it had bitten him.'

'I might conceivably buy that if you had a shred of evidence. Do you?'

'A handful of dust,' said Bognor lamely. 'Well, a cake tin of dust.'

Parkinson swore. 'I'm not in the mood for frivolity,' he said. Bognor reflected glumly that he never was. 'And I do not wish this affair to take up too much of the department's time.'

'No, sir.'

'If the dog did appear in Bogota and Cairo it would have had to be smuggled?'

'Yes.'

'So it could hardly have gone out in the normal way through a conventional airport?'

'Unlikely.'

'Whoever organized it would have had to have specialist knowledge of animal transport?'

'It's a reasonable assumption, yes.'

Parkinson stopped drumming the blotter and brought the side of his hand down sharply on the edge of his desk.

'For Christ's sake, Bognor,' he shouted. 'You're paid to make those sort of assumptions for yourself.' He stopped and then continued in a calmer vein. 'Kindly prepare a list of dog transporters or whatever they are, and I suggest at the same time that you make some sort of enquiry about Percy Pocklington and Eagerly. But this time, please curb your enthusiasm. It is not part of your job to go prancing about digging things up in the middle of the night. You invariably ball it up. Kindly confine yourself to asking questions and interpreting the answers.'

'Yes,' said Bognor, miserably.

'Now.' Parkinson leaned back and assumed the manner of a tutor who knows that his pupil is not only an imbecile but has also failed to do the work required. 'Why precisely do you imagine that these people have gone to such lengths to prevent you seeing the corpse of this damned poodle?'

'I somehow assume that it's because the dog died from rabies.'

'Is that logical?'

'I think so.'

'And yet when the Duchess's dog contracted the disease she was ready enough to inform the authorities?'

'She had to. It attacked her kennelmaid.'

'That doesn't follow. Your hypothesis is not logical. I do not believe that the poodle died from rabies.'

Bognor was confused and unconvinced. Then he looked at Parkinson and saw that he was wearing his smuggest expression.

'Do you have grounds for saying that?' he asked suspiciously.

'I might,' said Parkinson, smiling thinly. 'I should have told you earlier, but when the police were going through Sparks' effects at his flat, the telephone rang. It was a kennelmaid at Mrs Potts' by the name of Rose. It appears that she was in the habit of giving Sparks information from time to time, which helped him in his approach to canine matters of one sort and another.'

'And . . .'

'And, Bognor, I've arranged for you to take her out to lunch.'

'You've what?'

'You heard me.' He glanced at his watch. 'She'll be here in a moment or two. A coffee and a plate of spaghetti or an omelette will do, and I'm not going to sign expense claims for anything more.'

'Why me? Why lunch?' Bognor was plaintive.

Parkinson shrugged, a malicious half smile making him look, to Bognor, even more than usually loathsome. 'She wanted to see you. Wasn't keen to talk to anybody else. Evidently you'd made some sort of impression on her and now that poor Mervyn has passed away it seems that she has information she's prepared to divulge to you instead.'

'But I didn't even talk to her.'

'Perhaps that's why she's impressed.'

Bognor didn't reply. 'I'll keep in touch,' he said, 'if there's anything to keep in touch about.' He slammed the door behind him.

He recognized Rose as soon as he saw her in reception, though it was her girth rather than her face which prompted the recognition.

'Good morning,' he said, in his most avuncular manner, 'Miss . . .'

'Smith,' she said, 'but I'd like Rose better. Mr Sparks always called me Rose.'

'Good. Fine. There's a little place round the corner

where we can get a bit of Italian food. If you'd like that?'

She said she would and Bognor led the way down Victoria Street, to a small spaghetti shop he usually patronized when he was feeling hard up and greedy. Miss Smith ordered spaghetti and chips while Bognor, suitably shocked, had a lasagne and also, heedless of Parkinson's warning, splurged on a carafe of red plonk.

'Well,' he said, regarding her plump, amiable features with muted goodwill, 'what have you got to tell me?'

'It depends,' she said, looking scheming in a coy way.

'On what?' asked Bognor, lighting a cheroot and looking less avuncular. She smelt of stale poodle.

'Mr Sparks used to pay me for information.'

'Oh. Did he? Well, I'm very much afraid I can't pay you for anything I haven't had. If you expect to be paid you'll have to tell me what I'm paying for.'

She looked disappointed. 'What'll you pay?'

'What do you want?'

'Fiver,' she whined. 'It's less than Mr Sparks paid.'

Bognor looked in his wallet. He only had one five-pound note left, along with three singles. He sighed.

'If it's useful, yes.'

Their food and drink arrived. Rose attacked both with gusto.

'It's about Fred,' she said, mouth full of pasta.

'I was hoping it might be.'

'I think he was done in.'

'Done in?'

'Yes. I found him, you see, early in the morning. I'd seen him the night before and he was all right then. Full of beans, good wet nose, clear eyes, coat shiny. Nothing wrong with him, there wasn't. And in the morning there he was. He looked as if he'd been in pain.'

'You don't think it could have been rabies?'

'That's what Mrs Potts said you'd said. She laughed about it.'

'And you agree with her?'

'It wasn't rabies,' she said emphatically, jabbing a fork-impaled chip in his face. 'He was as sweet natured as ever he was.'

'What makes you think it was murder?'

'It was so sudden, that's why.'

Bognor was irritated. He watched her stuff another load of carbohydrate into her mouth and then said, 'Is that all?'

She finished her mouthful and drank, then wiped her face messily with a paper napkin. 'Nope,' she said, 'it's the day before which makes me think it was murder. I think it was something to do with Mr Cecil Handyside.'

'Handyside?' He grimaced. Another new name. Another wild goose or red herring to be chased or hooked. He had enough already.

'Handyside,' he said, 'who's he?'

'Nasty bit of work if you ask me,' she said. 'He's been round a lot lately, poking about. He runs "Animal Transport" at Andover. Mrs Potts uses him when she sells a dog abroad. He does it all. Gets the dog crated up, fixes all the licences and the clearances and takes the thing up to the airport. Breeds pugs on the side.' She sniffed.

Bognor was interested for the first time. 'And did he come on the day before Whately Wonderful died?'

'That's what I'm trying to tell you.'

'And . . .'

'They had this row. They didn't seem to have been getting on very well for a bit. I don't know why not. Mrs Potts didn't say, but I think he wanted her to do her domestic business with him as well. We always pack up ourselves if a dog's just going to somewhere in England. Or Scotland come to that. I mean, you only have to put it on a train and slip something to the guard. Or people will come and collect. It's no real trouble. Only I think Mr Handyside wanted to start some special delivery service with his own vans. Something like that. *Anyway,* the last time he came they had this terrible argument. Dreadful shouting and swearing and Mrs Potts pushing him down the path and him shaking his fist and saying he'd see her finished. Quite frightening it was, I can tell you.' She wiped up the final spots of tomato sauce with a piece of roll.

'When was that?'

'In the morning. Just after feeding time. Probably around eleven.'

A waitress came. Rose asked if she could have a slice of the gateau. He said yes and ordered coffee for himself.

'Are you suggesting Mr Handyside killed the dog himself?'

'Yes. He's got mean eyes. He'd do it all right.'

'But you've no proof.'

'No.'

'You think he'd do it just because Mrs Potts wouldn't join in with his dog transport scheme?'

She lowered her eyes and went red. 'Well,' she said, 'I don't know.'

Bognor lit another cheroot and pondered. If Handyside had been involved in the dog smuggling then perhaps he had been trying to persuade Mrs Potts to participate. And if Mrs Potts had refused to join in, then he would start to threaten her and if she persisted, some of those threats might have been carried out, in which case . . .

'Here you are, Rose,' he said impulsively. He took the last five-pound note from his wallet and handed it across the table. 'You've been very helpful,' he said. 'If anything else turns up don't hesitate to get in touch.'

Back at the office there was a message to ring the laboratory. He feared the worst and was proved right.

'Is this some sort of joke?' It was the senior analyst —McAlpine, a humourless technocrat whom he occasionally encountered in the canteen when a total failure of funds or very bad weather forced him to eat there.

'No. Why?'

'I thought this bloody cake tin of yours was supposed to contain the remains of a dog.'

'Not necessarily,' said Bognor, improvising rapidly.

'I was more interested to know whether or not it did contain the remains of a dog.'

'It doesn't.'

'Well, what does it contain?'

'Burnt newspaper, kindling wood and coal. All you have here, sonny Jim, is the embers of a household fire.'

'That's exceedingly interesting.'

'I'm delighted you think so.'

There was the abrupt click of a telephone receiver being replaced in anger and Bognor sucked his teeth. Another black mark. He would be bound to complain to Parkinson. At last, however, he had time to make one of his lists. He found a pencil in a drawer and began to write on a piece of lined foolscap.

After a minute he had a depressingly long list of names: Ailsa Potts, the Duchess of Dorset, Coriander Cordingley, Cecil Handyside, Percy Pocklington, Edgar J. Eagerly. He paused to chew on the pencil end and then added Albert Ramble, rival of Mrs Potts. It wasn't beyond the bounds of possibility that a man who was known to the world as Britain's second-best breeder of poodles might nobble the prize product of Britain's best breeder. Gardeners did it with vegetable marrows. It had been heard of with racehorses.

He stared long and hard at the list. The trouble with it was that it involved so much speculation, so much assumption. With an imaginative use of both he could involve every person on his list and a few besides. If Cecil Handyside was arranging the transportation of the dogs, Percy Pocklington could be the bent judge who made sure that they got the first prize every time, the Duchess was the producer whose dog had been used, Edgar J. Eagerly purported to be the owner of the dog for the purposes of the show. Coriander Cordingley used her travel and contacts to provide an intelligence network—as did Pocklington and the others. Albert Ramble and Mrs Potts were breeders who had been approached. It was a perfectly plausible theory and he resolved to try it out on Monica that evening.

He threw down the pencil with some satisfaction. It would help, he realized, if he knew a little more about the world of dogs. He stood up, stretched and went for a short walk.

Fifteen minutes later he was back with the *Dog Gazette*. It was a thirty-two page volume printed on indifferent paper, and for the most part in exceptionally small type. He flipped idly through it. Advertisements for dog shows were followed by advertisements for dogs. He had no idea there were so many breeds. He noticed that there were five brindle Afghan bitches for sale and that a minor Alsatian champion was at stud (fee £20). Most of the advertisements were for puppies for sale, or dogs willing to have sex. The second bit, indeed, was a little like one of those underground sex magazines except that instead of 'Virile company director seeks willing chick' you had 'The Chaldon Chows are now at stud for the winter. Champion Chaldon Chummy—fee 35 guineas—this dog consistently siring winning stock'. Cairns, chihuahuas, Finnish Spitzes, German short-haired pointers, Dobermanns, Groenendaels, Keeshonds, Lhasa Apsos, Norwegian buhunds, Schipperkes, Schnauzers and Shih-Tzus were all among those willing to have sexual intercourse for a fee. The money involved was not large. Bognor saw nothing more than fifty guineas. However, he supposed, if a dog was sufficiently famous he might demand more, and in any case one dog could presumably service several bitches in a day. At fifty guineas a go it surely shouldn't be impossible to make several hundred pounds on a brief visit to America, and if you could increase the fee the profit would obviously rise.

He turned on to 'Breed News' and stopped briefly at the 'Poodles' entry. 'I was very sorry to hear,' it began, in a typeface so tiny that even Bognor whose eyesight was formidable, had to screw his eyes up to read, 'that Ailsa Potts had lost her dog, Champion Whately Wonderful. Ailsa and I have had our ups and downs over the years and have disagreed over everything it is possible to disagree about. No doubt she will persist with the seaweed theory and allow Dutch clipping until she retires. But perhaps I am a bit of a fuddy duddy on things like this. Anyway Whately Wonderful was a great dog in the making and a great loss to dogdom. Many of us believed that he was the finest dog ever to come from Ailsa's kennels and I can say no higher than that. . . .' The tribute continued on its meandering and fulsome way for a further three paragraphs until petering out over a name he recognized immediately: 'Albert Ramble'. 'Hmmm,' he said to himself, and absentmindedly underlined the name on his list. He wondered. . . .

That evening he showed the magazine to Monica, while he was recounting the adventures at Piddlehampton. He told his tale as flatly and unemotionally as possible, while omitting any mention of the bed he slept in.

'So you staggered back to the hotel when you'd come round, did you?'

Bognor flushed. 'No, they drove me back and dumped me in my bed.'

She looked up sharply. '*My* bed?' she said. 'Why did you say it like that? Why *my* bed? Why not just bed?'

'Because it was *my* bed they put me in.'

'Of course it was.' She was looking at him with obvious suspicion. 'No one suggested it wasn't, until you.'

'I didn't . . . I only. Anyway, did you go out for that curry?'

'Yes, as a matter of fact.'

'Who with?'

'None of your business.'

He was irritated, as much with himself as with her. She went back to reading the magazine, sulking. He sat and stared. Then after a few minutes' petulant silence she said, 'Isn't someone called Percy Pocklington on your list?'

'Yes.'

'Olympia. Listen. Sounds super. "Grand Dog-lovers' League?'

'Yes. At least he runs the League, I didn't know he was quite so pompous about it.'

'They have a show tomorrow.'

'Oh. Where?'

'Olympia. Listen. Sounds super. 'Grand Dog-lovers' League Championship Show. Many classes, both open and obedience. Special displays by the Merioneth formation sheepdog team and the Rentadog Stuntsters. Guest appearance of Raffles, the Excelsior Chewing Gum Dog. Best of Show to be judged by Percy Pocklington and televised at home and abroad. Presentations by Miss Northern Hemisphere".'

'I might go to that. What time is it?'

'All day.'

'I'll turn up in the afternoon. Might learn something to my advantage. Certainly meet some of my protagonists for the first time. Would you care to come?'

'Not much.' She smiled, forgivingly, and Bognor wondered, with a twinge of jealousy, where she'd spent the night. 'But I will. On one condition.'

'Which is?'

'That we can have lunch at the Coq Hardi.'

'You're on.'

He couldn't afford it, he knew that. Not after the fiver for Rose, for which Parkinson would never reimburse him, but it was worth it for harmony. Besides, he enjoyed a good lunch.

5

Olympia was seething with dogs and people. A programme which Bognor bought at the turnstile claimed 7000 dogs and he doubted whether they outnumbered the humans. He and Monica stood just inside the hall staring about them, unsure where to start. All round the perimeter of the building there were little stalls like fairground booths. Some sold dog shampoos and dog deodorants, dog soaps, dog scents and canine *eau de cologne*. Others offered dog whistles too high pitched for the human ear or little fur lined dog jackets, dog motoring goggles or even dog—or rather bitch—chastity belts. The variety of canine comestibles was equally remarkable. There were dog chocolates of every description, not to mention biscuits and meat, pies and pastries and every sort of health food nutrient for dogs from seaweed à la Potts to Doggy buckwheat bread, dried nasturtium leaves and spun protein tripe.

'Let's start with all this,' said Monica, making straight for the 'Dog Drug Store'. 'I don't believe it,' she said, picking up a bottle which said 'Dr Merlin's heartburn pills—suitable for all breeds. Relieves indigestion swiftly. One pill for toys, three for large. Dose after meals'.

Bognor was examining scent. ' "*A bas les chattes*," ' he read, ' "an exotic odour particularly suitable for blonde or white coats. *Cher, cher, chien*—for the very special dog".'

Nearby there was a small electric toothbrush with a

label attached which claimed 'for the dog who has everything'. He winced. Slowly they wandered on, mesmerized by the anthropomorphic oddity of it all. Just beyond the MacDogs' stall which sold coats in forty-six different tartans he saw a discreet card advertising 'Coriander Cordingley's canine cameos—capture your pet in oils or watercolours. Twenty guineas head and shoulders, thirty for the whole dog'. Behind the card and surrounded by portraits of Alsatians, Pekinese, poodles and a striking group of three bassets, sat Miss Cordingley herself. She was, appropriately, in a tweed suit, and had a silver brooch of a labrador's head pinned to her lapel.

'Simon,' she said, smiling, 'how very nice. What a surprise!'

She had, he noticed, toned down the make-up but she still managed to look like a tart, albeit in a plain wrapper.

'How nice to see you,' he said, smiling back.

'Are you going to introduce me to your . . . friend, darling?' said Monica, frostily. Bognor did as he was told and the two women surveyed each other disapprovingly. He was sorry to see that Monica made her own dislike more obvious than Coriander.

'We met at the Duchess of Dorset's,' said Coriander. 'I'm afraid Simon wasn't well. He had an anti-typhoid injection which rather interfered with his performance.'

She managed to give the last phrase precisely the double meaning which Bognor wished to avoid.

'No, I'm afraid I wasn't really in full possession of all my faculties,' he said, making it worse.

Coriander laughed, huskily, and Monica said frostily, 'I'm glad to say he seems to have recovered now, Miss Cordingley.' Then added in a loud aside to Bognor, 'Come along. I want to see some dogs.'

When they had moved on, Bognor grinning a farewell to Coriander, Monica whispered to him noisily, 'She's a right bitch.'

'Shhh,' he said, crossly. 'Anyway, in these surroundings I think that's a compliment.'

Just as he spoke a be-tweeded lady in brown brogues strode past. Pinned to her enormous bosom was a rosette with 'Dog-lovers' League. Best of Breed' on it.

'There you are,' he said triumphantly, 'see what I mean?'

She didn't smile. Instead she pushed through the crowd towards the middle of the hall where, to judge from the yapping and the occasional flashing of cameras, the dogs themselves were competing. He was just about to burst out of a particularly thick part of the scrummage, when he realized that he'd almost trampled on a very small and elderly lady, once more, like all the others of her sex, clad exclusively in tweeds.

'I'm awfully sorry,' he began, then saw who it was. 'Why, your Grace, I'd no idea you'd be here, I thought you were in quarantine.'

She seemed no less surprised to see him. And not pleased either.

'Aha. Mr. Worthing.'

'Bognor.'

Perhaps it had just been the elbow he'd pushed in her face, but she did seem remarkably antagonistic. Still, the last time she'd seen him he was in the process of stealing an orange box from one of her flowerbeds. Maybe she was entitled to be hostile.

'We are not suffering from mumps,' she continued, 'the only people who are in quarantine are my dear Dandies.'

'May I please introduce . . .' said Bognor, casting around for Monica in the crowd, but not seeing her.

'Apparently not, young man,' said the Duchess, 'some other time perhaps.'

She bustled away, pushing through the crowds with an agility and determination which was surprising, considering her age and the fact that she only came up to most people's waists.

He found Monica among the Afghans. They were sitting or lying on narrow benches, owners' names and addresses pinned next to them along with the rosettes of the more successful. At intervals along the benches sat little groups of owners, a motley collection whose only common denominator was a deplorable scruffiness which contrasted dramatically with the impeccable grooming of their pets. Monica looked sad.

'It does seem a shame,' she said, 'such beautiful animals, like this. I feel like letting them all free.'

'I'd rather you didn't. Parkinson would have me fired for that.'

She laughed. 'Good job too,' she said, 'I'm even more tempted.'

'I've just seen the Duchess of Dorset,' he said. 'She was in a mood. Called me Worthing again. She only does it to annoy. She knows perfectly well my name's Bognor.'

'She obviously can't tell the difference. Can't say I blame her. I thought she couldn't go to dog shows. Surely she's in quarantine?'

'That's what I said. I think the point is that she's not in quarantine, only her bloody dogs. Still, I don't know why she should bother to come if she's not showing.'

Monica frowned. 'I wonder . . .' she said. 'You don't suppose she is showing?'

'She can't. It's against Ministry regulations. And the Kennel Club, come to that. It's not possible.'

'If she can break all the rules and show her animals in Colombia and the United States, surely she can do it here?'

It was Bognor's turn to frown. He said nothing but he felt the adrenalin begin to flow. They walked on a little way, through more benches containing Yorkshire terriers with their hair in curlers, and strange, almost fluorescent Weimaraners, described by the more adventurous breeders as 'Grey Ghosts'. Eventually they emerged into a show ring where a scrupulously neat gentleman in pin stripe suit was standing with his chin in his hands, trying to look knowledgeable. Around him there paraded a dozen or so small mustard-coloured dogs more or less under the control of a dozen or so assorted ladies, and one young man wearing a cloth cap and a pinkly self-conscious expression.

'My God,' said Bognor, 'Dandie Dinmonts.'

'Are you sure?' asked Monica.

'Positive,' he said. 'I'd recognize them anywhere. Look at those absurd top-knots on their heads and those bandy legs. Not to mention those beady little eyes and those vicious teeth.' He thought ruefully of his ruined suedes. 'You can tell from the way they walk that they've got weak bladders.'

'Oh, Simon!' Monica laughed, and he laughed with her.

'Do look at the judge,' he said, 'he's a hoot. He's wearing spats.'

It was true. He *was* wearing spats. Also an expression of truly ferocious determination. He was about fifty with a high complexion, crinkly black hair which looked too black to be true, and a monocle screwed firmly into his left eye. Rather short, he had a tendency towards chubbiness which would have made him look unbelievably pompous if it hadn't been for the spiv-like moustache which gave him a hint of raffishness.

'He's terrific,' agreed Monica, watching wide-eyed as the judge bent almost double, apparently trying to peer under the dogs' bellies—a quite impossible feat without actually lying down. 'Whoever can he be?'

A woman in a plastic mac, who was standing immediately beside them, said 'Shhh!' aggressively. 'It's Pocklington,' she whispered.

Bognor leant towards her. 'What? Percy Pocklington?' he said conspiratorially.

'Yes,' said the woman, looking at him as if he was mad. 'Where've you been? Haven't you seen him on the tele? He does the Meatibix ads. You must have seen him.'

'I'm sorry. No.' Bognor felt inadequate.

The woman grunted and turned back to the ring, leaving Bognor to unravel further mysteries for himself. Mr Pocklington was now examining three or four dogs in minute detail. He peeled back their gums to look at their teeth, he put his hands on a foreleg here, a muzzle there, ran a finger down the back of one animal's neck and spent several seconds caressing another's rump. It was most perplexing. Bognor's attention drifted to the ringside where the spectators looked horribly knowledgeable. Most, he presumed, would be owners either of dogs in the ring, or of others less successful. On the far side he saw the Duchess of Dorset, hunched over her walking stick. She looked smaller than ever and was watching with an intensity which seemed greater even than Mr Pocklington's.

Monica tugged at his elbow. 'Let's go,' she said, 'I've no idea what's going on.'

'I think it's almost over. In a second he'll declare a winner.'

'Can't think how,' said Monica, 'They all look the same to me.'

'He's an expert,' said Bognor, who'd been boning up on the *Dog Gazette*. 'He'll decide on the merits of the coupling, the spring of the ribs, the shortness of the stifle and the soundness of the temperament.'

'Oh really,' she said. 'How on earth can he decide about temperament just by looking down their throats for a few minutes? What a presumption. It's like asking me to decide on his temperament by watching him judge.'

'It depends on whether they give him a nip or a pee on his spats,' said Bognor. 'Anyway I've got a fair idea of his temperament just by watching him in the ring.'

This flippant and ill-informed discussion had distracted their attention from the events of the ring which had quickly reached a crescendo. Glancing up to discover the cause of the confused noise which had disturbed them Bognor saw that five or six enormous women had surrounded Mr Pocklington and were subjecting him to violent abuse. It was difficult to discover the precise nature of their complaints but he distinctly heard the words, 'cheat,' 'impostor' and 'fix.'

'What on earth's happened?' asked Bognor of the neighbouring expert in the plastic mac.

'He's given it to Millicent Trench's Tiresome Terrapin, that's what's happened,' she said, glaring at the confusion which showed signs of becoming violent. One stout lady was beginning to brandish a golfing umbrella.

'So what?'

'Millicent Trench never won a Best of Breed in her life,' said his informant disparagingly. 'Runted little dogs hers are. No wind and dreadful temperaments, hardly worth bothering with.'

'Then why's she won today?'

'That's what they want to know.' She gestured to the lynch mob which had quietened somewhat with the arrival of two officials who were standing authoritatively at Mr Pocklington's elbows. 'Either Percy P's made a bloomer or there's something fishy about it. If you ask me, there's something fishy. Why do you think Dora Dorset's looking so pleased with herself?' She pointed to the Duchess who still sat on a slatted wooden chair. There was no question about it. The Duchess was smirking.

Bognor was perplexed. 'I don't know,' he said. 'Why do you think?'

Plastic mac arched her eyebrows. 'I don't think that dog's Tiresome Terrapin any more than you're Gregory Peck. If you ask me, that's one of the Duchess's.'

'Is that possible?'

The woman shrugged, turned on her heel and pushed away through the crowd.

'You stay there,' said Bognor to Monica, 'I'm going to have a word with her Grace.'

He strode across the ring to the chair opposite and stood in front of the old woman. Suddenly he felt very angry.

'Why so pleased, Duchess?' he asked, conscious that he was being unnecessarily overbearing.

'Oh, Mr Worthing,' she simpered. 'How agreeable and how very soon. You're taking quite an interest in our little world of dogdom. Most flattering. I had sensed that in the matter of canine appreciation you were more than a little reticent, but I was evidently mistaken. How nice to be proved wrong.'

'I don't care about dogs, your Grace, but I do care about criminal practices, and I must ask what it is that gives you such pleasure.'

'Nothing criminal in taking pleasure, surely,' she said, her little eyes sparkling dangerously. She was tapping the floor with her stick and for an uneasy moment Bognor thought she was going to strike him across the shins just as she had belaboured her dogs when they'd been impertinent. 'Though we do have laws of trespass in this country. It's not so very long ago that people caught poaching were shot out of hand. Quite out of hand. But I digress.'

'Indeed you do,' said Bognor. 'I asked why you were looking so pleased with yourself and you still haven't answered me. I have heard allegations being made against you.'

'Young man,' said the Duchess, her voice shrilling. 'You are becoming tiresome. Your presence irks me. Millicent Trench is an old and valued friend. Naturally I take pleasure in her success. Great pleasure. Enormous pleasure. Pride indeed. Perhaps you wouldn't understand these things, Mr. Bognor. I doubt whether pride and pleasure play much part in the deliberations of the Board of Trade. Eh?' She had risen to her feet now and was bristling, whether from anger or excitement he couldn't tell. He wondered if she would have a stroke.

'Maybe not pride and pleasure,' he said, 'but I suffer from unshakable prejudice.' He was rather pleased with that but the Duchess bristled all the more. She made a strange guttural noise to convey displeasure and pushed Bognor to one side with her stick. As she did, a languid, drawling voice sounded around his left ear hole.

'Havin' a spot of bother, your Grace?' it said. Bognor froze, half expecting the karate chop with which he associated it. It was extremely like the voice of the man who had knocked him unconscious in the park at Piddlehampton Manor. He turned gingerly to confront the voice's owner and found a thin sandy haired figure with a red and white handkerchief knotted nonchalantly at his neck. He exhaled a pungent smoke through his delicately flared nostrils, which Bognor immediately identified as Balkan Sobranie.

'Don't think we've bin introduced,' he said, sounding just like a member of the BBC's repertory company in an adaptation of Trollope. 'Handyside. Cecil Handyside.'

'Bognor,' he replied. 'Bognor of the Board of Trade.'

'Charmed,' said Mr Handyside, breathing out more smoke and examining an exquisitely manicured fingernail. He wore a canvas Norfolk jacket, tightly belted to show off his tiny waist, but Bognor noted with satisfaction that his hair was thinning badly. Also that he'd cut himself shaving that morning. Just above the lip; nasty little nick.

'Do hope you're not upsettin' her Grace,' he said. 'Doesn't do to go round upsettin' people, 'specially not her Grace. The Duchess has had a lot to put up with recently. Her friends are beginning to be a little anxious on her behalf.'

'That's enough, Cecil,' snapped the Duchess. 'He's perfectly harmless. Good day, Mr Worthing.'

The two of them walked away, Mr Handyside lending the Duchess a supporting arm. Bognor smiled. He realized now that she called him Worthing to annoy but only remembered to do so when she was in control of herself. She reverted to 'Bognor' under stress.

The crowd around Mr Pocklington had dispersed now, the last to leave being a thin, delicate woman who was weeping copiously. A burly man who looked like a bucolic farmer was assisting her from the ring. Mr. Pocklington was left victorious, rubbing his monocle triumphantly with a spotless white handkerchief.

Bognor accosted the weeping woman and her escort with suitable diffidence.

'I'm sorry,' he said, 'to trouble you at a time like this, but I wonder if I might have a word?'

At first he thought they were going to brush past him, indeed the man did say, 'Some other time, can't you see she's upset?' but the woman interrupted him. 'I'm perfectly all right, and if it's the press I'm quite prepared to be quoted. Are you from *Dog News* or the *Gazette?*'

'Neither. I'm from the Board of Trade.'

'Oh.' They both looked disbelieving.

'Have you got time for a coffee?' he asked, hopefully. Again they stared at him in disbelief. Then the man nodded. 'Don't see why not,' he said. 'By the way, my name's Ramble, Albert Ramble. This is Mrs Protheroe.'

Simon introduced himself, and asked if he could meet them five minutes later in the main refreshment room. He had to tell Monica what he was doing. She was still standing where he'd left her, by the side of the Dandie Dinmont ring which was now filling up with beagles—pretty dogs with ugly owners, he thought as he circumnavigated them.

'That was fascinating,' she said. 'You seemed to be upsetting the Duchess more than somewhat. Who's the pouf with the egg-timer figure?'

'That's Handyside, the one who knocked me out at the Duchess's.'

'Oh, Simon. Really.' Monica grinned at him. 'You can't have blown very hard. He's an utter weed.'

'Appearances can be deceptive,' he said sententiously. 'He's got a very neat line in karate. Anyway, I can't stop. I'm having a coffee with a couple of breeders. I think I may be on to something. I'll see you back here in twenty minutes. Have a wander round and keep your eyes peeled.'

'O.K.,' she said. 'Don't be late this time and try to avoid having your coffee doped or your head smashed in by some crazed dog maniac.'

He smiled and kissed her. 'As if you'd care,' he said.

The cafeteria was scruffy and Bognor saw with a flicker of amusement that despite the theme of the day's events it was still advertising 'hot dogs'. The room was heavy with B.O. and cigarette smoke. After a moment's peering round he spotted Albert Ramble and Mrs Protheroe in a far corner near a sign marked 'Fire Exit'. He sat down between them and accepted the cup of tepid khaki liquid with an extravagant display of offering to pay, which Mr Ramble steadfastly refused. Bognor was impressed by the man. He had a strong, obstinate face with heavy bones and whiskers growing high on his cheeks. Bognor was always impressed with whiskers that high on a face, if only because he was physically incapable of growing them there himself. Mrs Protheroe was more nondescript but she was obviously almost hysterical with frustration.

'That bloody little woman,' she said as Bognor sat, 'everyone thinks she's so marvellous. Oh, Dora Dorset's so good for her age. Manages all on her own. Hardly any help. So friendly. So helpful. So kind. Ugh. She makes me sick. It's just because she's a bloody Duchess that everyone crawls about like that. She's not even old. She's not eighty yet, and that bloody stick's pure affectation. She'll be using an ear trumpet and a bath chair next. Bloody old woman.'

'Calm down, Sylvia,' said Mr Ramble, putting a hairy hand on her wrist. It was a very large hand. And very hairy. Bognor wondered how he'd get on with Cecil Handyside in a spot of unarmed combat.

'Hang on, I'm going to get us all a drink,' said Ramble. Before Bognor could remonstrate, he had shot off in the direction of the bar which was open and doing brisk business.

'Could you explain?' asked Bognor. 'I'm new to all this, and I haven't quite worked it out yet.'

Mrs Protheroe laughed shortly. 'I've been at it for seventeen years,' she said, 'and I haven't worked it out either. So I don't know what chance *you've* got.'

She lit a cheap filter cigarette and stared glumly at her coffee. To Bognor she seemed different—less robust than her competitors, more vulnerable. Perhaps it was just the tears.

'Can you start at the beginning?' he asked tentatively.

'If you like,' she said. There was a pause while she frowned, smoked a little and obviously collected her thoughts.

'We always had Dandie Dinmonts when I was a child,' she said. 'My father had a farm in the Cheviots and they come from there. They're really Cheviot terriers only they got called Dandie Dinmonts because of the farmer in *Guy Mannering*. He had one. I think it's a silly affectation myself. I'd much rather they were called Cheviots, but there we are. That's the official Kennel Club name and that's all there is to it.' She inhaled heavily again. 'I had a special one of my own. He was called Mustard. My elder brothers had Pepper and Salt so, of course, I had to have Mustard. Silly really, but you know what people are like. Anyway, I've had Mustard ever since.'

'How did you come to start breeding?'

'My husband died about eighteen years ago, and I had enough money to scrape by on, and the house had a couple of acres. It seemed an obvious idea. I know the dogs quite well and it's turned out quite successfully.'

Albert Ramble reappeared with three brandies. They thanked him and Bognor slipped him a pound note which this time he accepted with only enough protest to seem polite.

'*Very* successfully, Sylvia.' He turned to Bognor. 'The point is, in our game, Mr Bognor, there are always the flashy breeders, the big name ones, the ones that win the big shows and sell animals to kings and queens and film stars and get invited to judge all over the world. All that sort of caper. And then there's people like Sylvia and me. I breed poodles.' Here Bognor nodded, in what he hoped looked like a display of wisdom and knowledge. 'Now in all the years I've been breeding I've never had what you'd call an outstanding dog. But on the other hand I've never had a dud. All my dogs are sound. Now you take a woman like Ailsa Potts. She's always producing prize dogs. But to my way of thinking a lot of her so-called prize dogs are weak in the leg, they're pigeon-chested, their eyes give trouble and their temperament's poor. That's by the way. The dogs of hers you don't hear about are a shocking lot. Something terrible. That's what the poor public get fobbed off with. The ones that don't work out. Inbred genetic freaks they are. It's the same in other walks of life, I know. You get your flash harries and your honest johns. Sylvia and me, we're both honest johns, except for one thing, and that is that this year we've both got better than usual animals. One that could really do something. Mine's never going to be what Whately Wonderful would have turned out like, but it would have run it damned close—with an impartial judge. And Sylvia's little bitch may not be what Piddlehampton Peter was, but there's not that much to choose.'

Bognor was beginning to get the picture.

'What happened today then?' he prompted.

Mrs Protheroe resumed her story. 'Albert's quite right. It's very unusual and if you are being unkind you could say it was something of a fluke but this year Merriweather Minnihaha is as good as anything except for Piddlehampton Peter. And as you saw it was beaten by something of Millicent Trench's. Well, it's absolutely absurd. Millicent actually ought to be banned. She's slovenly, incompetent, ignorant. Well, not to put too fine a point on it, I think she's slightly mental. I'm not saying anything against her. She's just a bit cuckoo. And she could no more produce a dog like that one today than she could lay an Easter egg.'

'So what dog was it?' asked Bognor, knowing the answer already.

'I'm almost positive,' said Mrs Protheroe, 'almost positive that that so-called Tiresome Terrapin was actually one of Dora Dorset's Dandies. There's a way they have of carrying themselves which is almost unmistakable. You wouldn't notice and I doubt whether even Percy Pocklington could tell, but those of us who are in Dinmonts know almost by instinct. That's why there was such a fuss.'

'The others all agreed with you?'

'Oh, yes.'

'But did it deserve to win?'

Mrs Protheroe lit another cigarette and thought. At last she said, 'It's extremely difficult for me to be objective, you'll understand that. And I'm not saying for a moment that it wasn't a very nice dog, but I honestly don't think it was as good as Minnihaha. Wouldn't you agree, Albert?'

Mr Ramble, who had been very quiet, nodded agreement. 'No question in my mind,' he said. 'What's more, I think Percy Pocklington realized it. You could tell from his expression.'

'You're suggesting he did it on purpose? That he's corrupt, in fact?'

There was a very long silence, then they both nodded.

'Reluctantly,' said Ramble, 'yes. I'm afraid after a good many years of seeing Percy in action I'm compelled to say that, yes, I think he's not quite straight. I don't like saying it, but I'm afraid it's true.'

'It's not the first time it's happened.'

'I'm choosing my words, Mr. Bognor,' said Ramble, 'and I would say that if you entered a dog in any breed and you were up against one of Percy Pocklington's friends, then no matter how good yours was you wouldn't have much of a chance.'

'And in this case the Duchess managed to get one of her own dogs entered under Millicent Trench's colours, as it were. Is that possible? Technically I mean? There must be forms and things.'

'It's too simple,' said Mrs Protheroe. 'The Trench woman has a dog called Tiresome Terrapin. It has the same markings as a dog of Dora's. For the day Dora's dog becomes Tiresome Terrapin. If the Trench woman agrees, no one can prove anything. They may suspect, but they can't prove.'

'Not even an expert judge?'

Mrs Protheroe shrugged. 'I'm as expert as anyone when it comes to Dandie Dinmonts,' she said. 'I certainly know more about them than Percy Pocklington. But I still couldn't prove in a court of law that Tiresome Terrapin wasn't Millicent Trench's. So much of what goes on in dogdom is based on trust.'

Bognor nodded. 'So what happens now?'

Ramble grinned forlornly. 'Pocklington says he'll hold an enquiry. But since he'll chair it himself and choose the members it doesn't mean anything. It won't last more than a couple of minutes. To be fair to him it wouldn't make any difference if it were held before three appeal court judges. As we say, there's no proof. "Only reasonable grounds for suspicion", as they say, and plenty would say the grounds are unreasonable. But what's the use of that? You'll never find them guilty. Even if we appeal to the Kennel Club it's still impossible to prove.'

'As far as I'm concerned,' said Bognor, 'the grounds are reasonable enough and in my book I'll accept a verdict of not proven.' He got up to go.

'By the way,' he said, 'what do you know about Cecil Handyside?'

Ramble and Mrs Protheroe looked at each other, raised their eyebrows and turned back to Bognor, both managing to convey by their expression that Mr Handyside was a very bad lot indeed.

'You certainly seem to have discovered the seamier side of our little world,' said Mrs Protheroe. 'What exactly is it that you are investigating? We've been blathering on about our problems but we don't know what yours are, do we?'

'You've been a great help, both of you,' said Bognor in his best Dixon of Dock Green style. 'Let's just say I'm investigating skulduggery. Dark deeds in doggy places. Killers in kennels. Things that go bump in the night. If you hear anything evil which could interest me, please ring me.'

He gave them both a card and said goodbye. By the time he returned to the rendezvous, the beagles were dispersing and Monica had vanished. He frowned, then sat down on a slatted trestle chair to collect his thoughts and look at beagles. They had the softest, kindest faces, he thought, as he gazed in their direction. So unlike those terrifying terriers. It was strange to think of such gentle looking creatures being used for hunting. He was musing on this when he was aware for the second time that day of Balkan Sobranie and impossible aftershave. Something like Yves St Laurent for men, he supposed.

He wrinkled his nose and looked up. It was, as he'd expected, Mr. Handyside.

'Thought I'd better seek you out,' he said. 'Just in case the Duchess's good manners deceive you.' He sat down on a chair next to Bognor and stretched his legs out in front of him. 'Pretty beasts, aren't they?' he said, waving his cigarette in the direction of the beagles.

'Just what I was thinking.'

'Ever been out beagling, Mr. Bognor?'

'No.'

'You should, Mr. Bognor. Wonderful exercise, and all the excitement of the chase.'

Bognor examined the manicured hands from narrowed eyes, and wondered if they were appropriate weapons for karate or other forms of unarmed combat. They were pretty but scarcely formidable. Mr. Handyside noticed.

'The dogs become quite transformed, hunting,' he said quietly. 'One minute as docile as you please. Next, they catch a glimpse of that hare and they're savage killers. They'll tear it limb from limb. I find it fascinating. Nature red in tooth and claw—all that sort of carry on. They say the hare feels no pain, but I can't believe that. What do you think, Mr Bognor?'

Bognor shrugged. 'No idea,' he said.

Mr Handyside smiled at him, with an expression he would probably have described as sardonic and which, Bognor reckoned, had been practised at length before a looking glass.

'It's the same with people,' he said. 'I remember in the Borneo campaign, when I was with the Marines, they'd become quite excited at the thought of blood. Gurkhas are the same, really rather mild-mannered little men until they unsheath their kukris. Did you do National Service, Mr Bognor?'

'No.'

'I thought not. Appearances aren't always deceptive.'

'You were with the Marines?'

'Commandos, yes. Some people seem surprised but

I'm sure you're far too intelligent a judge of character to be surprised.'

Bognor appreciated the menace in the man but found him too disagreeable to be really alarming.

'Are you warning me off?' he asked.

Handyside lit another Sobranie and sprawled deeper into his chair.

'That's a sadly crude way of putting it, Mr Bognor,' he said. 'And I wouldn't dream of warning off a servant of Her Gracious Majesty when he's on official business. All I'm saying to you is that dogdom is a private world where we all get along perfectly nicely by minding our own business. We don't awfully like nosey parkers and trespassers.' He blew smoke in Bognor's direction. 'Legitimate curiosity is quite gratifying, but snooping is something else altogether. Ain't it?' He lapsed back into the affectation which his threatening tones had partially obscured.

Bognor grinned back, irritated. 'I'll be careful,' he said, 'but I suggest you exercise a little more discretion yourself. For example, you weren't exactly exuding sweetness and light when you called on Ailsa Potts the other day. Strangely over-excited by all accounts.'

The revelation went home. For a second Mr Handyside looked dangerously rattled, then he relaxed again. 'You know,' he said, 'some of my friends in the dog world have already opined that you're not half so harmless as you look. I've been giving you the benefit of the doubt. Perhaps I was wrong.'

'Perhaps.'

The conversation was too artificial for someone of Bognor's temperament. He disliked the self-consciously cool, with their nuances and that maddening habit of leaving the most important part of every sentence un-expressed. Now he found himself being manoeuvred into the same laconic style and it upset him.

He was about to leave Mr Handyside to his manner-isms when there was a crackling of static electricity and an announcement came over the public address system.

'We very much regret,' said a voice, which through

the dehumanizing of the loudspeakers still sounded very much like Percy Pocklington, 'that owing to unforeseen circumstances, the appearance of Raffles, the Excelsior Chewing Gum Dog, has had to be cancelled. Instead, at very short notice, Mrs Gertrude Patty of the Parisien Poodle Parlour in Peckham will give a display of clipping and coiffure. Thank you. I am also instructed to say that entry number thirty-three has withdrawn from the terrier judging. No substitutions allowed. Thank you.'

The news meant less than nothing to Bognor but was evidently important to Mr Handyside, who immediately stood up, flung down his cigarette in a peremptory fashion, paused to grind the stub under his heel and said, 'Have to be off. I do hope we'll have no more tiresome to-do's, Mr Bognor. *A bientôt.*'

Bognor watched the departing dog transporter with relief. He disliked him, and he was afraid that, deep down, he was scared of him too. He was certain now that it had been his pampered hand which had rendered him unconscious, and the knowledge chilled him. Unfortunately he was no nearer proof of any kind. Also, Monica was missing. He had better go in search.

They almost collided five minutes later, saved only by the intervening presence of a Pyrenean mountain dog which interposed its considerable bulk between them.

'People!' said its owner, in accents of infinite contempt, as the dog gave an angry growl at being thus sandwiched.

They apologized, and the woman marched away, grumbling about the superiority of dogs over humans.

'I've been peeling my eyes,' said Monica, kissing him on a cheek. 'There are some funny goings-on going on. Let's find a quiet corner and I'll tell you quickly.'

It was easier said than done, but eventually after pushing and shoving through the increasingly sweaty throng, they found a deserted bench by the borzois.

'I got bored of waiting,' she said, 'so I wandered off to see the Rentadog Stuntsters. Rather disgusting, actually, dogs walking tightropes and jumping through flaming hoops. Anyway, I was watching a display when I saw the Duchess talking to your girl friend, Coriander. It seemed to me that the girl was ticking the Duchess off in no uncertain manner. Then Percy Pocklington came up and all three of them had a terrific discussion. There was another peculiar looking woman with a green felt hat as well and she seemed to be backing up the Duchess but in the end I think they must have lost because she looked frightfully cross. They all split up and the Duchess left.'

'What? Left altogether?'

'Yes. She left the hall. She's gone home in a sulk, I should say. And then there was the announcement, which must give the reason.'

'What announcement? What reason?' Bognor was confused. Everything was moving too fast.

'About the Dandie Dinmont being withdrawn. Tiresome Terrapin, the dog that won the class. You know you went off to talk about it.'

'Yes. I just didn't connect,' he said. 'They didn't say anything on the loudspeaker about it being the Dinmont. It just said number thirty-three. How do you know it was the Dinmont?'

'I asked some doggy type. Everyone's heard about it. Apparently it's the talk of the show. The official reason is that the silly animal's got some eye infection which has suddenly flared up, but as my doggy type said, it would hardly have won its class if it had been oozing pus out of one eye.'

'So?'

'So informed gossip is that the Duchess and Millicent Trench were working out some sort of fiddle and got cold feet when someone called Mrs Protheroe lodged an official protest. Is that your weeping lady?'

'Yes,' said Bognor, 'only the real force there is Albert Ramble. Did your man say anything else?'

'He'd heard about you. Apparently you're the source of some gossip as well. The dog people are on the alert. He said he'd heard that there was a full scale government enquiry going on into what he called "irregularities" in the dog game. According to him the Special Branch had been called in. I suppose that means you.' She giggled.

'It's not funny,' he said. 'I suppose it must.'

Once more the loudspeaker system cut across their conversation.

'Judging of the Dog-lovers' League Dog of the Year will commence in five minutes in the main ring. The finalists are the Siberian eelhound, the pointer, the Sealyham, the Dalmatian, the St Bernard and the Yorkshire terrier. Judging will be by Percy Pocklington, Esquire, and the prizes will be presented by Miss Northern Hemisphere. Please remember that all proceeds from this show go to the Dog-lovers' League, the world's premier organization for man's best friend. Please give generously. Thank you.'

'Let's go and watch,' said Bognor. 'I'd like another look at Percy Pocklington. As far as I can gather most of the proceeds from the show go to him and the League is the world's premier organization in aid of Percy Pocklington. However, we shall see.'

The crowds were already gathered round the main show-ring in anticipation of the day's highlight, and their journey there was therefore easier than expected. When they arrived they had difficulty in seeing anything at all, but by standing on a bench, and then on tiptoe, they could just make out one corner of the arena where the six dogs were already formed up with their handlers.

'I don't like the look of your Mr Handyside,' said Monica, peering over the pork pie hat of the short Eton cropped lady in front of her. 'Who's that elephantine woman he's talking to now?'

'Where?' asked Bognor. His view was not as clear owing to the great height of the Eton cropped lady's friend who was immediately in front of him.

'There.' Monica pointed to the ringside seats immediately beyond the Siberian eelhound. Bognor did a little jump to see better and almost upset the bench. The two lady friends turned round and clicked their tongues in exasperation. 'Sorry,' said Bognor, blushing. He and Monica changed places briefly and he saw that Handyside was gesticulating almost frenziedly to no less a person than Mrs Ailsa Potts of Three Corners, Surblington. Handyside looked agitated and Mrs Potts was purple and beetle browed. As he watched he saw that she was talking in single words and he guessed from her expression and the pained faces of her neighbours that she was blaspheming. She was clearly enraged but the object of her fury was not Mr. Handyside. She was not swearing at Mr Handyside, but with him. He was nodding in agreement, and the up and down motion of his head reminded Bognor irresistibly of a snake about to strike.

'Nasty,' he said to Monica, changing back to her place. 'That's Mrs Potts, whose poodle started me off on this shaggy dog story. The last time they met they were having a monumental row. Now they're agreeing about something. And very heatedly. If my theory is right they should be having blows.'

He was prevented from further conjecture by an outburst of clapping. From their position it was impossible to tell what had provoked it, but a few seconds later the competitors set off in Indian file and disappeared from their limited field of vision.

'That must have been for Pocklington,' said Bognor. 'Do you imagine he's still wearing his spats?'

'He looks the sort of man who'd wear spats in bed,' said Monica. She peered in the direction of the ring. 'I can't see anything,' she said.

'Even if you could you wouldn't understand it.'

'True.'

'Shhh,' said the lady with the Eton crop.

They took to silence. After a while Monica whispered to Bognor, 'They're back.'

'Who?'

'The dogs.'

Now the loudspeakers resumed. 'Our six Dog-lovers'

League finalists will now parade individually,' said the speaker. 'First the eelhound.'

There was a further outbreak of clapping interspersed with cheers and the odd boo.

'I'd no idea everyone took it so seriously,' said Bognor. 'I've never heard of an eelhound. What is it?'

'It looks rather like an anteater from here,' said Monica. 'Very long nose, I suppose for catching eels with. It's rather fun.'

There was a pause while, presumably, Pocklington did his examinations, peered at the animal's bone structure and assessed its personality. Then the loudspeaker announced the pointer and the applause was repeated. So the ritual continued, with each dog being introduced in turn. Then they ran about a little more, before the loudspeaker announced, 'The judging is now completed. Here to present the prizes and to award the Dog-lovers' League Challenge Trophy for this year's championship is Miss Northern Hemisphere. A big hand, please.'

More dutiful clapping and several whistles.

'She's vast,' said Monica, 'Her bust's as big as your Mrs Potts'.'

'Not so droopy, I hope,' said Bognor.

'Very bouncy,' said Monica. 'I wonder how she does it? Quite a feat of engineering.'

Eton crop turned round and put her finger to her lips. The loudspeaker began again. 'I shall announce the first three dogs in reverse order. Third . . .' pause for effect '. . . the Sealyham.' Applause and quiet while, presumably, the beauty queen appended a rosette.

'Second, the Dalmatian.' The same noise and silence followed, but whatever was happening was still out of their sight. 'First . . . the Siberian eelhound.' After this the applause was thunderous, the silence more prolonged. Finally there was further cheering as the winner did a lap of honour, part of which they could see.

'Well,' said Bognor, 'I suppose that'll increase popular demand for eelhounds. I want to see if I can have a quick word with Pocklington. If he's involved in this he'll be warned about me by now. If not he may be able to shed a little light. I want to see what his account of Bogota and Cairo is.'

Monica agreed and they set off in the direction of the arena. Before they got there, however, they met Mrs Protheroe and Albert Ramble. They still seemed disconsolate.

'At least you had the dog thrown out,' said Bognor.

'It retired,' said Ramble. 'It should have been disqualified, then Sylvia could have been declared winner and gone into the terrier judging.'

'But we agreed you couldn't *prove* anything.'

'Maybe,' said Ramble. 'Anyway it didn't make much odds. He got his own protégé the cup.'

'How do you mean? He doesn't breed eelhounds.'

'As near as dammit. It's an open secret. He more or less imported the breed himself after the Moscow dog show a few years ago, and the principal breeder is Doris Pink. She used to be the assistant secretary of the Dog-lovers' and he set her up. I think she was his mistress though it's hard to imagine now. Paying for her kennels was his way of getting rid of her. Mind you, I can't prove that either.'

He smiled, and for the second time they said good-bye with renewed promises to get in touch should anything turn up.

They found Percy Pocklington in the enclosure behind the Dog-lovers' League stand, where he, the triumphant eelhound, its owner, and sundry other dog-lovers were drinking non-vintage Mumm champagne. From time to time he and the dog and Miss Pink would pose for the photographers clustered just outside the enclosure. He looked like a man who had cast off the worries of the day and was now basking in the achievement of a job well done.

At the gate of the enclosure a bullnecked steward, wearing a Dog-lovers' League lapel badge, barred their entrance. Bognor remonstrated and produced his card. The man went away to consult his chairman and came back shortly with an invitation to both of them to take champagne with Mr Pocklington. Both of them disliked Mumm—it was too sweet and reminded Bognor of his late great-aunt's marrow wine—but they accepted.

'At last, Mr. Bognor,' said Pocklington, greeting them with a jarring demonstration of false bonhomie. 'I've heard so much about you from my friends.'

'Favourable, I hope?' said Bognor, accepting a glass of wine.

'Cheers,' said Mr. Pocklington. He ignored the question. 'Always a relief to get to this stage,' he said, 'without any serious mishap. The only setback this year has been Raffles, the Excelsior Chewing Gum Dog. Still, I gather he's insured for several thousand. Besides, security's not our problem. That's admin.' He sniffed complacently.

'What happened to Raffles?' asked Monica.

'Disappeared. Owner left him for five minutes while he went to have a pee. Next moment he'd gone. We've got plenty of witnesses. Couple of chaps turned up, bold as brass, wearing white overalls, and just carted him off. Everyone thought they were officials.'

'That sounds cool,' said Bognor. 'Why should anyone want to kidnap Raffles, though?'

'Ransom, I'd imagine. He's too well known to be any other use. Even a layman would recognize him.'

'I wouldn't. I don't even know what sort of dog he is.'

Mr Pocklington clearly didn't believe him, though Bognor was quite serious.

'He's a bulldog,' he said. 'White with black markings. Very distinctive.'

'Who owns him?'

'A syndicate control the agency. One of them's my friend, Cecil Handyside, whom I gather you know. There are five of them altogether. Anyway,' Mr Pocklington was suddenly in a hurry to leave, 'what can I do to help?'

'A couple of questions, that's all,' said Bognor. 'I

can see you're busy. First I wanted your views on the shows in Bogota and Cairo, Illinois. It's been suggested that the Dandie Dinmont which won those two prizes might have been one of the Duchess of Dorset's dogs and not what it claimed. What do you think?'

Pocklington rubbed his spivvy little moustache with the index finger of his right hand. The movement was intended to suggest thoughtfulness, but Bognor was certain the judge wasn't thinking. He'd had his reply ready for days.

'Don't misunderstand me,' he said, eventually, 'I don't wish to speak ill of the dead, but I understand you got your information from Mervyn Sparks. Perfectly sound judge, Mervyn—at least of our four-footed friends. But when it came to bipeds he let his prejudices run away with him. He never liked me. Jealousy mostly. He used to get plenty of assignments but usually because I couldn't accept them. Now I'll wager all Lombard Street to a china orange that he tried to implicate me in this affair. Am I right?'

'Up to a point.'

'Thought as much.' He scratched his chin in the same phoney way that he'd dealt with his moustache. 'I know my dogs, Mr Bognor, and I can tell you I was surprised to find a Dinmont so far south as Bogota, but if anyone can afford that sort of money it's Edgar Eagerly. More important, though, I know my people, and Edgar Eagerly wouldn't stoop to malpractice. He doesn't have to. He's worth a fortune. No, no, you're barking up the wrong tree, if you'll excuse the metaphor.' He laughed immoderately, spilling the champagne from the flat, saucer-shaped glass.

'But I've heard it suggested that the dog—to a connoisseur—was obviously one of the Duchess's. Carriage, character, er . . .' Bognor trailed away into silence, unable to think of the appropriate terms.

'It's true,' said Pocklington, 'that Dora Dorset's dogs are usually easy to recognize, but that's because they're better than anybody else's. They conform to the breed standard with an exactitude which others find impossible to match. And Edgar's dog was as good as some of the Duchess's. But then Edgar is one of the world's leading experts in genetic engineering, and when I taxed him with Dora Dorset he admitted that his dog's grandfather had been one of Dora's. The mother had been from Canada and I gather she'd got some Piddlehampton blood in her too. So up to a point it's true. Anything else?'

'Yes.' Bognor wasn't satisfied, but as before he felt out of his depth. 'What about this afternoon's little episode? I'm told that Millicent Trench has never won a competition in her life and scarcely knows one end of a dog from the other.'

'Calumny,' said Mr Pocklington. 'Millicent has been a League supporter for twenty years. She's branch secretary for South West Surrey. She knows as much as any Dandie Dinmonter around, and as far as I'm concerned it is surprising that she hasn't had more success earlier.'

'But the dog withdrew?'

'I can't comment on that. The enquiry reached no official decision because we were pre-empted, but even if it had, the League's rules forbid further discussion on that too. I've no idea why the dog withdrew but I regard it as most unfortunate. In my opinion it would have run the eelhound very close. That eelhound has remarkable depth of rib but I'm not happy about the way he goes behind.'

'Oh,' said Bognor. 'So as far as you are concerned Tiresome Terrapin was Millicent Trench's own dog?'

'I've absolutely no reason to suppose otherwise, Mr. Bognor. If I could give you a word of advice I'd pay no more attention to Mrs Protheroe than you have to. Unsound temperament. Strong suggestion of inbreeding. Pity. If we approached human breeding with half the knowledge and discipline that we bring to dogs then the world would be a better place. And now if you'll forgive me I must return to my guests.'

Bognor grudgingly forgave him and they joined the departing crowds jostling out into the down-at-heel purlieus of Kensington's nether end.

'Happy?' asked Monica on the way home.

'Not in the least,' he said.

6

Next day was Sunday but it brought little rest. As soon as he woke, Bognor reached for his bedside pencil. He had been troubled in sleep by strange dreams of packs of rabid eelhounds, demented Duchesses and dog-lovers. Wearing only spats, he had been pursued by this throng across Hyde Park until, cornered in Queen Mary's Rose Garden, he had been attacked with empty champagne bottles. It was then that he woke.

For an age he lay sucking the end of the pencil and looking for some clue he had failed to appreciate. Beside him Monica lay snoring lightly. He wondered if he should wake her, but it was only just seven, so instead he went to the kitchen to make coffee, found a pad of lined foolscap and began to write.

'Champion Whately Wonderful,' he started, 'was murdered by a person or persons unknown not long after Cecil Handyside had had a flaming row with Mrs Potts.' He stopped and sucked at the pencil. 'That's a theory,' he said optimistically, and wrote again. 'Cecil Handyside killed him. Next day Coriander Cordingley exhumed the deceased's orange box after I'd left, removed it to Piddlehampton Manor where the corpse was re-buried by the Duchess of Dorset. Later on, Handyside hit me on the head and somehow I was transported to the hotel.' He left out the bit about being transported to Coriander's bed for fear that Monica should read it. 'Now,' he muttered, still sucking, 'that makes Handyside a killer and the other two accom-

103

plices. So if Piddlehampton Peter was smuggled out to America the odds are that Handyside and Coriander were involved along with the Duchess.' He flung down the pencil in exasperation. Parkinson would not be impressed. It remained pure speculation. He made the coffee and then wrote down Percy Pocklington's name. Against it he entered: 'Awarded first prize to dubious Dinmont in Illinois and Colombia; to eelhound in which he has an interest; made suspect Tiresome Terrapin best of breed.' All that suggested that Pocklington was corrupt, but then Pocklington's whole appearance and demeanour suggested corruption. Bognor would have convicted him on the grounds of the spats and the moustache alone. The connection between Pocklington and the others was tenuous, to say the least. Of course he knew them but in dogdom everyone knew everyone else. That much Bognor already realized. He passed on to Mrs Potts. She was guilty of deception, that much was certain. She had prevented Bognor from examining the corpse and had refused to answer questions. He pencilled, 'Why deceive me?' against her name and by a ridiculous piece of auto-suggestion began humming the 'Lass of Richmond Hill'. 'Guilt or fear,' he pencilled. She was either an accomplice or she was a victim. If the dog had been murdered then she was a victim and therefore frightened. If it had been merely gastro-enteritis or a haemorrhage or rabies then she was an accomplice. But if it was any disease or illness *but* rabies there was no point in concealing it. Besides, Rose had suggested murder and he had a hunch that Rose was more perceptive than she appeared. She'd been right about Handyside. He'd definitely been upset when he mentioned the argument with Mrs Potts.

'What *are* you doing?'

It was Monica, still dishevelled with sleep. 'It's frightfully early. Come back to bed,' she said.

He looked at her, undecided, then reckoned that the prospect was insufficiently inviting.

'I'm making lists,' he said, 'but it's not getting me

far. You go back to sleep and I'll go and get the papers and bring you breakfast in bed.'

She smiled. 'You *can* be quite nice,' she said grudgingly.

The newsagent's was a hundred yards down the street on the corner. He ambled there, hands in his pockets, wondering how he was going to solve this case. As usual he was dimly aware that there was an obvious and vital clue which he had completely failed to spot. Perhaps something would turn up. It usually did.

He bought an armful of papers and ambled back, idly perusing the sports page. The news was, as usual, disastrous. The England side had totally collapsed after a brilliant start. It was, he reflected, very ignominious to be taught the finer arts of cricket by Indians and Pakistanis. Back at the flat he gave all the papers to Monica, and boiled eggs. The toast he burnt at the first attempt, but browned adequately at the second.

'I see the Chewing Gum Dog's been kidnapped,' said Monica, when he took the food in. 'Your friend Handyside's had a ransom note. They want £10 000.'

Bognor put down the tray, whistling, and picked up the paper. It was one of the populars and alongside a large picture of the crotchety old bulldog there was an account of how two kidnappers had abducted Britain's most famous dog. He found the tale heavy going for the prose was florid and the puns atrocious. However it transpired that before leaving the Dog-lovers' League Show last night Handyside had received the demand which had been handed in to one of the commissionaires. The commissionaire, who had been dealing with a disorganized crowd scene at the time, had only the dimmest recollection of who had given him the letter. He thought it was a man of medium height with mouse-coloured hair, between about twenty-five and forty. Bognor laughed drily. It didn't look as if they'd find *that* man in a hurry, and it was nice to see Handyside getting a taste of his own medicine. Serve him right. He was about to give the paper back when his eye caught an item in the Stop Press.

'Surblington sex fiend strikes', he read. It had been the name of the town which had attracted his notice. 'Police were searching the Surblington area for the killer of a twenty-one-year-old Rose Smith, a kennel-maid, whose body was found late last night dumped in a lonely lovers' lane outside the town. She had been sexually assaulted.'

'Look at that,' he said, throwing it down on the bed. 'The Stop Press.'

'How ghastly,' she said when she'd taken it in. 'That's your informant? The one you gave the five pounds to?'

'Yes.' He thought of the fat girl shoveling spaghetti and chips into her capacious mouth. 'I'd better get down there right away.'

'But it's Sunday.'

'She's dead and I have a shrewd idea who killed her.'

'Who?'

'Handyside.'

'Oh, Simon, come *on*.' She laughed. 'Where have you been? That man is as queer as a cream puff. The paper says she was sexually assaulted. That means rape or worse and that must rule out that horrid little pansy. He couldn't possibly have done it.'

Bognor shrugged. 'I think he's a psychopath,' he said, 'and everything is beginning to point in his direction.'

'How do you mean?'

For answer he went to the kitchen and came back with the foolscap pad, the gist of which he repeated to her.

'Pure speculation,' she said. 'This wretched girl was obviously on her way back from the flicks or from some hop and she was picked up by a sex fiend as the paper says and raped and dumped. It happens all the time.'

'What if Handyside found out, as he did, that she'd told me about his row with Ailsa Potts?'

'He might be upset,' said Monica, 'but I doubt whether he'd kill her.'

'He'd already killed the dog, remember . . .'

'Speculation.'

'And yesterday before the final judging he was having that very curious conversation with Mrs Potts. Agreeing with each other. Now the only thing they're likely to agree about is the awfulness of Rose, the informer. Mrs Potts said as much to me when I first met her.'

Monica looked thoughtful. 'I still think you're assuming too much,' she said.

'Good God,' he said, 'you sound just like Parkinson. I have to make assumptions. I have no proof yet, but if I go down to Surblington and talk to the local police I may be able to find some.'

'Oh, all right,' she said, 'only try to be back for lunch.'

He was back in time for lunch. The local police had been obstructive to the point of bloodiness. He had tried unsuccessfully to telephone Parkinson for support but without that even his faithful Board of Trade Identity Card had been useless.

The CID man had heard him out. Just. A lot of nose-picking, watch scrutinizing, and clumsily suppressed yawning had gone on, but he had sat through Bognor's speech. Then, when it had come to its conclusion, he'd said, 'Thank you for coming, sir, very kind, though you needn't have troubled. We'll keep you informed of any development since she was a Ministry contact.'

To begin with Bognor had retained his politeness. 'I'm sorry, Inspector,' he'd said, 'but I don't think you quite understand. I'm asking to be involved in this investigation and I'm suggesting that you question Mr. Handyside as soon as possible.'

The Inspector, at least ten years his senior, had looked at him scornfully. 'I doubt whether we'll find that necessary in view of the circumstances . . . sir. It's evident that this was a straightforward sex crime and had nothing whatever to do with matters concerning dogs. If you'll pardon my saying so, a great deal of what you've told me sounds like pie in the sky. And if I might make so bold, I'd also suggest that if a third party were to overhear the allegations you've just made then Mr Handyside would have a sound case in law for any action he might choose to take.'

'Inspector, please try to realize this is a matter of national importance.' He'd realized as he said it that the policeman would merely laugh. He did.

About this point he lost his temper, which was unfortunate. The altercation which followed was short but bitter and some of what Bognor said he regretted. However he objected to being laughed at.

Furious at the lack of response to his approaches, he had gone straight to Three Corners to interview Mrs Potts. When he arrived he was told, by a lachrymose colleague of the dead girl, that Mrs Potts was at Mass. The idea of her being a Catholic had not occurred to Bognor, especially after the macabre performance of the dog's funeral, but he settled down to wait by the front gate, after establishing from the kennelmaid that Rose had last been seen on her way to the evening performance of a film called *Bat Out of Hell*. The epic seemed familiar to Bognor though he hadn't seen it. She had been on her own and the bus stop was five minutes' walk away. The road was unlit. It had all been too easy.

After half an hour Mrs Potts arrived, accompanied by the police inspector with whom Bognor had dealt earlier. Another short sharp row ensued and ended with the policeman warning him off.

'If I see you nosing around on my patch again I'll have you booked for obstructing the course of justice,' were the words used. Bognor had been so angry that his only retort was 'Balls', which in the circumstances was hardly adequate. The whole embarrassing incident had been made worse by the presence of Mrs Potts who watched his ignominious defeat with undisguised satisfaction. Her flabelliform features were smudged with what a stranger might have assumed to be tears, but Bognor, cynically, decided that such was not the case.

After shouting 'Balls', he had driven straight home. Which was why he was back in time for lunch.

'I can't say I blame him,' said Monica over beer and cheese and chutney sandwiches in the local pub. 'It must have sounded pretty silly to him.'

Bognor was not amused. 'Closed minds,' he snapped. 'That's what he's got and it's what you're developing too. I've a bloody good mind to go straight to Handyside's now and have the whole thing out with him.'

Monica coughed on a cheese sandwich. 'That way,' she said, 'you really will end up in trouble.' She drank more beer. 'However, if you felt adventurous you could ask him some harmless questions about the chewing gum animal and his ransom. That would be a legitimate thing to do. He could hardly sue you for that.'

'I don't want another argument with some idiot of a policeman,' said Bognor ruefully, 'but I'm damned if I see why I should be messed around like this. The more I think about it the more convinced I am that the girl was murdered because she was telling tales out of school. Her frightful old boss knew what she was up to. She was livid when I appeared on the scene in the first place and even more when she realized that it was her kennelmaid who was acting as an informer.'

'She could hardly have done it,' said Monica drily. 'It was rape, after all.'

'Don't be sick,' he said. 'It's too much of a coincidence for her to be murdered so soon after that conversation. It all hangs together. What's more there's something very suspicious about Raffles and his disappearance. I don't know what it is but it seems too clear cut to me. It was too easy. Surely someone would have stopped two men kidnapping Britain's most famous dog?'

'Evidently not.'

'Not evidently at all.' He wiped froth from off his upper lip. 'You're quite right. Handyside can't sue me for asking questions about the ransom. Let's go and pay him a visit.'

'What? Now?' Monica's pint was still half full.

'Now. While I'm in the mood.' He stood up and wiped crumbs off his trousers.

'But it's miles,' wailed Monica, 'I wanted a quiet afternoon, reading the papers.'

'Andover will take about an hour and a half,' said Bognor, decisively, 'the country air will do you good.' He reached out for her glass and drained it in one gulp. 'Come on,' he said.

'I don't see what you're going to achieve,' said Monica petulantly as, yet again, Bognor drove west.

He shrugged. 'If I'm right,' he said, taking both eyes off the road in front of him and only just replacing them in time to see a pair of red traffic lights, 'and he did murder that wretched kennelmaid, then his nerve has failed—even if it's only temporary. I want to jostle him a bit when he's in a panic. I also want to have a look at his operation. See how he might smuggle dogs in and out.'

They were on the motorway now, cutting through the fir trees near Camberley. They would be in Andover in less than an hour.

'Smuggling them out isn't much of a problem, surely?' said Monica. 'It's getting them back in again. I mean there are no laws about the export of dogs. Only bringing *in* unpleasant diseases. He could quite easily send out dogs in a conventional export order and only do real smuggling on the way in.'

'You need an export licence,' said Bognor, frowning. 'But you're right, the real problem *is* getting the dogs back in again. Still, as I said before, if you can do it with people you can do it with animals. My guess is they fly in to France or Belgium or Holland and come across to the south coast in some fishing boat.'

'Sounds complicated.'

'It would be. There's money involved.' He paused and switched topics. 'I suppose Raffles would be insured?'

'Bound to be.'

'So if he were kidnapped, Handyside and the syndicate would collect?'

'Yes.'

'And if they'd arranged the kidnapping themselves?'

Monica gazed out of the window at the traffic returning from a weekend by the sea. It was building up already. 'Then,' she said, 'they would either destroy the dog, in which case they would only collect the insurance money. Or if they were being very greedy they would smuggle it out of the country and flog it there to some unscrupulous continental advertising agency.'

'I agree,' he said. 'It will be fascinating to see how far his nerve's gone.'

'If his nerve *has* gone and your theory's right I suppose the dog will turn up safe and well, any minute now.'

'I suppose so.'

They relapsed into silence. At Micheldever junction after the motorway ended he took the right fork towards Andover, then shortly before the town he had to brake suddenly when he saw a large wooden hoarding by the road side. It was a simple black and white sign which said 'Animal Transport Ltd. ½ mile left'. He turned down the twisting lane for the requisite distance and then saw a modern bungalow surrounded by a complex of wooden sheds, also new. In the yard outside the house stood several vans and one larger truck, all clearly marked 'Animal Transport Ltd. Prop. C. Handyside'.

'Never imagined he would live in a bungalow,' said Bognor, driving slowly past and peering in as he did.

'What are you looking for?'

'I don't know. Signs of life, evidence of guilt . . .'

'I wonder if your friend, Coriander, will be here? She seems to make a habit of popping up wherever we go.'

Bognor said nothing. Instead he backed into a gateway a hundred yards beyond Château Handyside, and turned the engine off. Finally he said, 'What do you think?'

'Nothing much. It looks like what it is: a small company which specializes in transporting dogs about the place.'

'Do you think I should go in?'

'Not much point in coming all this way just to look over the front gate.'

'No.' He paused. 'I tell you what though. You stay here and if I'm not back in half an hour, get hold of Parkinson and tell him what happened.'

'Aren't you being rather melodramatic?'

'I hope so.'

He got out and sauntered back down the lane. It was still warm and the recent dry weather had baked the mud and dung on the tarmac to a dry crust. The only sound was birdsong, which as usual he couldn't identify, and the dull hum of traffic from the main road. When he reached the bungalow he looked at his watch. He would give it twenty minutes. There was a brass dolphin on the door and Bognor took its nose and banged twice. He thought he saw a corner of lace curtain twitch in the room immediately to his right. Then, a moment later, the door opened and Cecil Handyside stood before him clad entirely in blue denim and wearing a single brass curtain ring in one ear.

'What do you want?' he said, making no gesture of welcome whatever. From behind his feet there came a snuffling noise like a pig rooting and Bognor glanced down briefly and remembered that he was supposed to breed pugs as a sideline. There was only one pug with him at the moment. He wondered where the rest were.

'I'd like a talk,' said Bognor.

'It's Sunday.'

'Well?'

'I'm tied up.'

'It won't take long.'

'Wouldn't it have been easier to telephone?'

'I wanted to have a look at your operation for myself,' said Bognor, easily. He had the impression that Handyside's nerve had failed.

'I'm only just back from Heathrow,' said Handyside,

'and what with one thing and another I'm really very busy.'

'Could I have a quick look round?'

Handyside sighed with exaggerated exasperation. 'I said it's Sunday. There's no one else here. We don't work on Sundays. I'm all on my own. There's nothing to see.'

'I'd still like to see it,' he said, 'I mean your vans for instance, I'd like to see inside one.'

Handyside looked pained. 'If you insist,' he said, 'but it's a bloody waste of time.'

They looked in one of the vans, which was a conventional small Ford with a grille behind the driver's seat and a few wire cages scattered in the back. Then Bognor insisted on looking into one of the sheds. Handyside agreed but with even more reluctance. He was now increasingly fidgety and kept glancing at his wrist to see the time. He talked very little but kept emphasizing the straightforwardness of his business, and said most of his animals were sent by sea since there was no hurry for most. Air freight charges were much greater. Apparently the main problem of sea travel was that dogs were frequently allowed to jump on hatch covers during the voyage. When the vessels reached port the hatch covers were removed but the dogs in true Pavlovian style continued to leap at them and fell down into the hold killing themselves. He'd lost a great many dogs like that. Bognor laughed slightly and Handyside looked pained. Just as he finished the explanation there was a noise of a car outside. Then another car. Then two together. At this point Handyside looked very agitated indeed and ran out to the yard. By the time they arrived the car or cars had gone.

'I really must ask you to leave now,' said Handyside. 'I have a lot to do.'

'I thought you didn't work on Sundays.'

He frowned. Bognor persisted. 'Just two final questions,' he said. 'First, what were you doing at Heathrow?'

For a second Handyside looked very worried indeed. 'Sending off a dog, of course,' he said.

'Whose? Where to?'

'I can't discuss that sort of thing, Mr Bognor. It's confidential. I picked the dog up from a client in Windsor, crated it and took it on to the airport. That's all.'

Bognor wasn't satisfied but he could check it. 'The other question,' he said, 'is could I please have a look at your ransom note for Raffles?'

'The police have already looked at it.'

'Maybe. I'd like to see it too. Do you object?'

Again an exaggerated show of reluctance was followed by grudging acquiescence. Still Bognor wasn't invited in but he saw from his watch that his twenty minutes were almost over. Much better wait on the doorstep. The piece of paper with which Handyside finally returned was a grubby blue sheet covered with letters cut from a newspaper. Bognor held it up to the light to read the watermark.

'Baildon Bond,' said Handyside drily, 'and the letters are cut from *The Times* and the *Daily Mail*.'

'Oh.' Bognor knew that made it impossible to trace. He read the words. 'Raffles returned within 24 hours receipt of £10 000'. There followed a name and address of a bank in Zurich together with a lengthy code number which Bognor assumed to be the account. It told him nothing at all and he knew that the Swiss bankers would say nothing either.

'Thanks,' he said, 'you've been very helpful. By the way, do the police think they'll get your dog back?'

'They're not optimistic,' said Handyside.

'Oh.' Bognor allowed himself the luxury of a supercilious smile. 'I do hope he was insured.'

'Yes, thank you. Goodbye.'

'Goodbye.'

The door slammed shut the moment the words were uttered, and Bognor stared at it speculatively for a second before returning to the farm gate where he'd left Monica. He whistled as he walked, aware to his surprise that the tune was 'An English country garden'.

Odd how one's subconscious produced apt clichés so easily. It was still as quiet as when he'd walked in the other direction half an hour earlier, though some of the heat had gone. Birds still sang, traffic hummed in the distance and Bognor thought how agreeable it would be to motor slowly back to London, stopping for a quiet pint of ale in a picturesque pub from which they could watch the final overs of a village cricket match on the green.

He had been musing along these lines when he suddenly realized with a shock that he had passed the gate by which the car was parked. That was odd. He picked a sprig of cow parsley from the hedgerow and frowned. Very odd. Turning round he retraced his steps for a hundred yards until he came to the gate once more. There was no sign of the Mini or of Monica. Still puzzled rather than alarmed, he climbed on to the gate to sit and wait. She must have got bored. Then he remembered the sound of the cars while he and Handyside had been in the shed together. The memory made him anxious but he was still reasonably sanguine. He sat on the gate toying with the cow parsley and wondering whether Handyside had lost his nerve. And if so how much. After another ten minutes he heard an engine and leapt down on the gate ready to upbraid Monica for alarming him unnecessarily. But it was only a Land Rover driven by a burly local. The man raised an arm in ritual salutation and Bognor waved back. He was really worried now. What's more he was stuck. He couldn't walk in the direction of the main road because if he did he would have to pass Animal Transport Ltd and he certainly didn't want to be spotted by Handyside. If he walked the other way he'd lose Monica.

He was on the point of risking a confrontation with the evil dog transporter when he heard the sound of his Mini. It was instantly identifiable, for it sounded, particularly when driven too fast, like a lawnmower in pain. Just now it was being driven too fast.

He jumped down off the gate narrowly escaping death as his car skidded to an erratic halt.

'Thank God you're here,' said Monica, 'I was terrified you might have been raped.' She was flushed and excited.

'Don't be ridiculous.' His anxiety had quickly become irritation and even envy now that he realized she was enjoying herself. 'Where have you been? I've been waiting for ages.'

'Hop in,' she said, 'I'll drive. I've developed a taste for it.'

He hesitated, then opened the door and sat down heavily in the passenger seat. Monica let out the clutch and they jerked off, far too fast. He wrestled anxiously with his seat belt, then turned to her as she attempted to slide round a double hairpin bend.

'For God's sake, slow down and tell me what you've been doing.'

'Giving chase,' she said, slowing slightly as they grazed the bank. 'I'm right in thinking that your girl friend has a white Morgan?'

'If,' said Bognor, 'you're talking about Coriander Cordingley, then yes, she has a white Morgan. At least she uses one. Why?'

They had rejoined the main road now and Monica was driving in a fashion which bordered on the discreet.

'About five minutes after you went off this little white sports car came round the bend . . .'

'From this road?'

'No, the other way. It must be a short cut. Anyway it slowed as it went past and I could see there was a tarty blonde driving. She looked a bit taken aback to see the Mini and after she'd gone past I saw her look in the mirror. Either she recognized me or the car because she suddenly accelerated like mad. Then she must have done a U turn in the yard because she came racing back past me again as if she'd seen a ghost.'

'The ghost of Whately Wonderful, perhaps. I wonder if poodles are given to haunting? Or Dandies come to that?'

'Don't be silly. Anyway she was obviously extremely anxious not to be recognized so I thought I'd go after her. Luckily the roads were very windy and I more or less kept in touch until Micheldever, then it got straight so she escaped. Jolly fast, those little Morgans.'

'And what,' asked Bognor, realizing that he sounded like Parkinson, 'were you going to do if you had caught her? Not that you had any chance in this old crate.'

'Given her a piece of my mind,' said Monica truculently. 'No, seriously, I'd simply have asked her what the hell she was so ratty about. I mean her behaviour was highly unorthodox and it needed explaining. I should have asked for an explanation.' She pouted and Bognor laughed.

'I'll bet it was to do with Raffles,' he said. 'That man is getting edgy. Still, if I'd murdered a kennelmaid I'd be edgy. I wonder what else she knew.'

Monica smiled. 'I think it's time you had a lucky break in this case,' she said.

The break came that evening, late. They'd stopped off for a drink by the Thames at Cookham and then gone round the corner for dinner at Bel and the Dragon. At home, all thoughts of dogs were banished by the last of a bottle of Hine and the first movement of the Pastoral. They were happily snuggled on the sofa when, as the first notes of the second movement began, the telephone shrilled a discordant accompaniment.

'Sorry to trouble you at home and at the weekend but it's Watherspoon.'

It took Bognor a few seconds to remember who Watherspoon was. The name itself seemed insufficient excuse for the disturbance.

'Watherspoon from the Kennel Club,' said Mr Watherspoon, aware of Bognor's amnesia.

'Of course,' said Bognor. 'Very nice to hear you again. What can I do for you?' Out of the corner of his eye he was dimly aware that Monica was undressing. He found the idea disturbing.

'It's about the chewing gum dog,' said Mr Watherspoon, 'the one that's been kidnapped. We've got some facts. It appears to have turned up in Copenhagen.'

'Copenhagen?'

'Yes. I thought you might be interested. You see Percy Pocklington's in Copenhagen for the Danish championships. I thought there might be a connection . . . in view of what we discussed before.'

'Yes.' Bognor was trying hard to concentrate, aware that Watherspoon's news was important but also that Monica, who'd had more to drink than he'd realized, was now naked.

'How do you know about Raffles?'

'We had a call from one of our contacts. There's nothing about Danish dogs he doesn't know, though he's a bit commercial for our taste. Apparently their biggest advertising agency was approached. It was done very discreetly but there's not much question that the dog they're trying to sell is Raffles.'

'Will they buy? I mean, the dog's stolen.'

'There's no extradition treaty in the world that applies to dogs. Besides they won't buy him as Raffles. They'll pretend it's a quite different animal. That won't matter. It's a trained TV performer, and everyone will recognize it from the chewing gum ads. They go all round the world.'

Bognor renewed his efforts of concentration, made even more difficult by the fact that his naked girl friend was sitting on his knee now, and kissing his left ear lobe. She was too old, he reflected, for this sort of caper, and too pudgy. Still, it was disconcerting. He pushed her away.

'Is your man sure?'

'As sure as he can be. The markings are very unusual. Like so many of these things it would be impossible to prove it in a court of law, but he's virtually certain.'

'Has he seen it?'

'Yes. He's retained by the agency. Well, he's retained by everyone in Denmark when it comes to dogs.'

Monica had gone to the bedroom in a sulk. Concentration was easier. 'He's not dealing with Pockling-ton?'

'That would be too much to hope for,' said Wather-spoon. 'I think your friends are cleverer than that. The dog's with a breeder near Odense called Larssen. Larssen, of course, is an old friend of Pocklington's. In fact he's the Danish representative of the Dog-lovers', but you can't make much out of that. Almost everyone in dogdom is an old friend of Pocklington's.'

'That's all fascinating,' said Bognor, meaning it. 'I'm tempted to fly out and have words with your Mr . . .'

'Winterfeld. Jorgen Winterfeld. I'm sure we can ar-range that.'

'Fine. We'll see. I'll ring in the morning if I may.'

He put the receiver down. A trip to Copenhagen might be rather jolly. Acres of naked flesh and willing ladies. The thought of it all reminded him of Monica and with a twinge of guilt he remembered that he'd snubbed her. He had better go and make up to her.

He was just beginning to make up to her when once more the phone rang. 'Leave it. I love you,' said Mon-ica, gripping his ear in her teeth and refusing to let go. He bit her back harder than he'd meant, and she gave a little yelp. 'Pig,' she said, releasing him. 'That hurt.'

'Sorry,' he said, 'duty calls.'

It was another break this time, though coming so soon after Mr Watherspoon's phone call it was a break of a perplexing nature.

'Handyside,' said a voice, which seemed to have gained a lot of poise and assurance since Bognor had last heard it, 'I thought I'd let you know we've found the missing Raffles. You've been so touchingly con-cerned for his welfare that I thought you should be among the first to know.'

'How did you get my phone number?' asked Bognor, irritated.

'You're in the book. Only one London Bognor has the initial S.'

Bognor swore under his breath. He'd asked the Post

Office to make him ex-directory but they constantly forgot. He would have to change his number.

'I'm delighted,' he said. 'How did you find him? What happened?'

'Some children discovered the poor old boy just wandering the streets of—Fulham—I think it was. They recognized him at once, of course. His markings are quite unmistakable.'

'So where is he now.'

'They turned him over to the Richmond Dogs' Home. I'm going to pick him up tomorrow morning. I thought we'd have a little celebration so I've asked the press along to witness the happy event.' He was drooling self-confidence now. It made him positively unctuous. 'Perhaps you'd like to join us? Eleven o'clock. Champagne perhaps? It would be so nice to see you again.'

Bognor flinched. 'Eleven o'clock at Richmond Dogs' Home. I'll be there.'

'Super,' said Mr Handyside. 'Good night.'

After this fond adieu Bognor sat holding the receiver in his hand while he pondered. When he put it down and went back to the bedroom he was still as bemused as before.

'This afternoon,' he said, 'we had no Excelsior Chewing Gum Dogs. Tonight we have two. How do you explain that?' He sat on the end of the bed and picked at his toenails. "It's very curious. I think I may have to go to Copenhagen.'

'For Christ's sake, come to bed,' shouted Monica. 'I'm fed up with waiting, and I'm no longer interested in your *bloody dogs*.'

7

Parkinson was not enthusiastic about Denmark.

'The only reason you want to go there,' he said, with deplorable predictability, 'is to see disgusting films. *Memoirs of a sex mad dentist; Danish blue*. Before we know where we are you'll be telling me that your precious Mr Handyside is selling dogs to the pornography industry.'

'I should think that's highly probable,' said Bognor, who had once been shown a lurid booklet in which people were depicted in unrepeatable and improbable poses with Alsatians. Parkinson ignored the remark.

'Before we have any expensive ideas about foreign travel,' he said, 'I suggest you travel to Richmond, which I believe is accessible by the Underground railway, or Southern Region or by one of London Transport's attractive red omnibuses, and establish the identity of the animal there. Your return fare should be no more than 50 pence which is the sort of budget I regard as appropriate.'

'How will I know if it is Raffles or not?'

Parkinson withered him with one of his looks.

'Even I, Bognor, would recognize Raffles, the Excelsior Chewing Gum Dog. Even I am aware that it is unusual, to say the least, to find a white bulldog with a black eye patch and a black foreleg and a precisely marked black crescent on its chest. And even I know that even if such a dog were to have a double it is highly unlikely that such an animal would be able to

121

sniff out Excelsior Chewing Gum in preference to the gum manufactured by anybody else. Let alone chew it.'

'That's what Raffles is supposed to do?'

Parkinson thumped the desk. 'Where have you been, man? Don't you watch the television?'

'Not much, no.'

Parkinson buried his face in his hands. When he removed it, he said simply, 'Please just establish the identity of this dog in Richmond. Then report back. But,' and here he raised his voice, 'do absolutely nothing else. Do *not* get involved. Do *not* make a fool of yourself. And report back on your return.'

Bognor smiled wanly and left.

Before catching the Underground he telephoned Heathrow airport's cargo centre and eventually found the official who'd dealt with Handyside's transaction the day before. After much prevarication from him and a judicious mixture of threatening and wheedling from Bognor, results appeared. Handyside had, it seemed, delivered a dog for despatch to Copenhagen. At this Bognor's heart started to pump extravagantly. Then the man said that the dog in question had been a bulldog, and Bognor became almost hysterical.

'Could it possibly have been . . .'

"I can guess what you're going to say, sir, and there's no question of it. We've been on the alert naturally ever since Raffles was abducted, and even someone like Mr Handyside can't be above suspicion, we know that . . .' Bognor could picture the bureaucrat's face, the ponderous, pompous expression as these flat clichés came rolling out.

'How can you be so sure?' he asked. 'Because it wasn't chewing gum, I suppose.'

Offence had been taken. 'Raffles is a white dog with some highly distinctive black markings, sir. This dog was jet black with no trace of white on its coat whatever.'

'Are you certain?'

'I'm a very busy man, sir, and yes I am certain and now I have work to attend to if you'll forgive me.'

Bognor didn't forgive him. So near and yet so far. There must be something in it. As he understood it Handyside had put a bulldog on the flight to Copenhagen and, within hours, Raffles was on offer in Denmark. In London the dog had been jet black and yet the dog which was on sale was apparently white with black markings. And the dog in Richmond was also white with black markings. Highly distinctive black markings at that.

He realized with a start that it was getting on for 10.30. If he was to make Richmond by eleven, using public transport, he would have to hurry. He ran out of the office and jogged breathlessly to the St James' Park station where, luckily, the first District Line train was Richmond bound. After Earls Court the crowds who had forced him to travel that far in a standing position dispersed to some exhibition or other and he was able to continue seated. Richmond was the last stop on the line so that he had ample time to think, but think as he might he could see no easy solution. Someone, to coin a phrase, was being sold a pup, but he couldn't yet see how or who.

There was a taxi waiting by the town station and he took it, regardless of expense, because he was late. The driver grinned when he said, 'Dogs' Home.'

'Some do up there, eh?' he said. 'I had a couple of boys from the *Express* earlier. Said they've got Raffles up there. Lucky he didn't end up as pet food if you ask me.'

'How do you mean?'

The driver laughed. 'They only keep the strays a week, then they flog 'em off, make them into canned meat. Or melt them down for soap.'

They were driving up Richmond Hill now, with its pretty, dolls' house-like shop fronts and its Georgian terraces leading away to the left. On the right, a long way below, a clear blue Thames threaded lazily through the green of the valley. At the top of the hill, by the park gates, the driver turned sharp left and pulled up outside a red-brick compound which looked like a Victorian gaol. A khaki van, labelled BBC Television, was parked on the double yellow line by the main gate.

The presence of television crews reassured him. He was in the right place. He marched in past a notice which said 'There is no Welfare State for animals, please give generously' and another in pseudo-childish handwriting, adorned with paw-marks, which appealed 'Please help build a new home for us dumb friends'. Inside the front hall he started to ask for directions at the reception desk, but before he'd finished the woman behind the grille said, 'Press conference first floor turn left third door on the right' and continued knitting.

The press conference, when he reached it, was attended by about thirty journalists. The reporters were standing around, faintly embarrassed at having to attend such a clearly silly-season event while the photographers crowded about the dog. This, wearing an expression of Churchillian hostility, was sitting on a giant Excelsior Chewing Gum carton and was flanked by two nubile ladies wearing platform heels, bikinis and sashes emblazoned with the one word 'Excelsior'. It undoubtedly had markings of the requisite kind but its general manner was one of surly belligerence which Bognor found surprising in a dog so famous. He supposed it might have something to do with the photographers' flashlights which kept exploding just in front of the animal's face, but the celebrated Raffles was surely used to that by now. The only person he recognized was Handyside who had taken off his ear-ring and had reverted to the casually knotted neckerchief.

'All's well that ends well, Mr Bognor,' he said, shaking hands and simpering. 'The villains must have panicked when they realized what a hue and cry had been unleashed. Besides it would have been quite impossible to have disposed of dear Raffles short of . . . Well, we needn't go into that, need we, old boy.' He leant down and made as if to stroke the back of the dog's neck, but before he could, the dog growled and snapped at him. Handyside withdrew the hand quickly and one or two of the journalists tittered.

'He's had a shock,' said Handyside. 'He's not used to being kidnapped.'

'I suppose,' said Bognor, 'that if the thieves had been imaginative they could have got rid of him abroad?'

Handyside showed no reaction. 'Most unlikely,' he said. 'It's so extraordinarily complicated unless you know the ropes. Besides these particular villains were interested in ransom money, not selling.'

'Still,' Bognor persisted, 'if they'd kept their nerve they could have had both.'

This time he thought Handyside seemed momentarily uneasy. 'In theory,' he said, 'in theory yes, Mr Bognor. But in practice I think not. I think you should meet Brigadier Willoughby, the Home's secretary.'

He introduced the Brigadier, a bluff brigadierly caricature who at first glance seemed more suitable for the secretaryship of a golf club than an animals' home.

'Board of Trade, eh?' he repeated after Handyside had gone off to explain that Raffles would not chew gum for the television cameras as he was still technically in a state of shock. 'Knew a chap in the Board of Trade once. Fellow called Parkinson.'

'He's my boss,' said Bognor.

'Good God, I wouldn't have thought he was old enough to be anybody's boss. That dates me. So you're in *that* branch of the Board of Trade,' he continued, removing the pipe from his mouth and jabbing it in Bognor's direction.

'Yes.'

'So you're here officially?'

'Sort of.'

'Ah.' The Brigadier sucked on his pipe. 'You got a moment,' he asked, 'when this lot's over? At least, I tell you what, this chap Handyside's laid on some sparkling white plonk or other which I don't suppose you'll want anything to do with. I've got a bottle of Gordon's and some bitters in my den, so we can slip out for a moment and have a pink gin and a chinwag while these blokes are laying into their vino. How

about that? You don't want to listen to Handyside
waffling on, do you?'

Bognor said that the last thing in the world he wanted
to listen to was Handyside's speech, so the minute the
two bathing belles with the sashes started to move
round with trays of sparkling white wine and packets
of chewing gum, Bognor and the Brigadier beat a discreet retreat.

'Well,' said the Brigadier when he'd mixed two very
stiff gins. 'Glad you showed up. This is much more your
sort of pigeon than the police's. May not be anybody's
pigeon but I'd like to tell someone about it. Burden
shared is a burden . . . er . . . well never mind. Cheers.'

He consumed the first half of his glass. 'Know anything about dogs?' he asked.

For what seemed like the millionth time in the past
week Bognor confessed his ignorance.

'Nor did I,' said Willoughby, 'until this job came up.
But I've had to do my homework and I reckon I know
as much as most now. Well, of course, I recognized
this dog as Raffles the minute he came in. He was
found up in Fulham and the people brought him
straight down here. We're better known than the police
when it comes to this sort of thing. Well, the second
we got him I rang Handyside. I'd seen his name in the
papers so I knew who to get in touch with. That was
fine. No problem. He sounded very relieved and said
he'd like to fix up a little party so I said that'd be O.K.
and that's what's going on down the corridor. So, you
might think all's well that ends well, eh?'

'I suppose so.'

'Yes, well that's where you'd be wrong. Have another gin?' He poured two more. 'Now after I'd finished
talking to Handyside I went down to have a look at
this Raffles creature. Not every day you get a dog worth
thousands in here. Most of the wretched beasts have
got distemper or virus hepatitis or leptospira canicola.
So I went down to the cells and I had a good look at
him, and the more I looked the less I liked what I saw.
Know why?'

Bognor gave an impression of deep thought and then shook his head.

'Nor did I at first,' said Brigadier Willoughby, clearing his throat noisily, 'but I definitely sensed that it wasn't the dog I'd seen on the gogglebox. It was a bulldog all right, and the markings were the same, but it wasn't holding itself well. Drooping. And the breathing was poor. At first I put this down to the ill effects of its kidnap, then I had another dekko at the coat. I had an impression that those famous markings were just a little too good to be true. Know what I mean?'

Bognor nodded cautiously. 'I think I see what you're driving at.'

The Brigadier smiled. 'I can see you're one of Parkinson's boys. Well, to cut a long story short, that dog had been faked.'

'Faked?'

'Faked. Tampered with. They used to do it a lot in the last century. Clip the tails to make the dog do better in competition, cut a bloodhound's eyes to make them droop more.'

'Whatever for?'

'Bloodhound's eyes are supposed to droop. Don't ask me why, ask the Kennel Club. The specification for the breed says that the eyes shall droop and those Victorians used to make them droop artificially if they couldn't do it naturally. But I'm digressing. Another common sort of faking was to whiten the animal's coat with magnesium. And it's that or something very like it that's been done to that dog out there. If we were to go back to Handyside's party now and scrape away at the so-called Raffles' coat I'd wager that within a few minutes you'd have revealed a totally black bulldog. Scarcely a white hair on him.'

'I see.' Bognor's mind was working overtime. 'I didn't notice it. The coat looked perfectly natural to me,' he said truthfully.

'Done by an expert,' said the Brigadier. 'No question about that. Take a naturally suspicious chap like me to spot it. And a very knowledgeable fellow too. Those press johnnies back there would never twig. Too gull-ible and too pig ignorant.'

'But someone like Handyside,' said Bognor, 'he'd notice, surely?'

' 'Course he would. He knew the dog too, so he'd be bound to spot an impostor. Anyway I realized what had happened late last night and I can tell you I was on the verge of telephoning Handyside to put him off and say someone was playing an elaborate practical joke, but . . .' Brigadier Willoughby fumbled with his matches and Bognor waited while he relit the pipe. 'Something made me leave it. Can't work out what it was. Some sort of hunch, I suppose. So I kept quiet and let him come round to work it out for himself.'

'And he came and didn't notice,' said Bognor, falsely naive.

'That's one possibility I won't accept. He'd decided that dog was Raffles before he'd even seen it. Hardly looked at it. Just walked in and said, "So there you are, Raffy, old man" and gave him a piece of cheese.'

'Cheese?'

'Yes. All dogs like cheese. Now. You're the detective wallah, what do you make of that?'

'If what you suggest is correct,' said Bognor, choos-ing his words, 'then there are only two possibilities. One is that Raffles has always, as it were, worn make-up so that he'd appear unusual and distinctive. And the second is that the dog giving the press conference isn't Raffles at all, but someone else disguised as Raffles, and that Handyside knows.'

Bognor recalled the pure black bulldog on the aero-plane to Copenhagen.

'No reason is there,' he asked, 'why it shouldn't be done in reverse? White dyed black, I mean.'

'Easier, I would imagine,' said the Brigadier.

'And it could be washed off again fairly fast?'

'Depends what sort of dye or paint you used. You on to something?'

'Could be,' said Bognor. 'Did you say anything to Handyside about this faking?'

'I'd left it too late,' said the Brigadier. 'If I'd said the dog was a fraud after he'd "recognized" it, then I'd have been calling him a crook or an imbecile. And I wasn't going to do that. Besides, he'd have blustered his way out of it. If he wants to carry on this sort of charade that's his business. It's not an offence. It's a bit like going to the lost property office when you've had your umbrella pinched. You collect the first umbrella you see. Doesn't matter whether it's yours or not. All part of the game.'

'That still doesn't explain why the dog was faked,' said Bognor. 'It sounds like an elaborate job. It would have taken a long time and a lot of skill.'

'Had to put on some sort of show for the press and the public,' said the Brigadier, swirling the remains of his gin about in the glass. 'I mean, if photographs of a black bulldog with no markings had appeared in the papers, not even you would have thought it was Raffles.'

'I suppose not,' said Bognor. 'But what it comes down to is that Handyside's dog—or the syndicate's dog—was stolen and still is stolen. And yet Handyside has accepted some second-best animal, pretending that it's the genuine article. Why?'

'That's your problem, old boy,' said the Brigadier. 'All it means is that the fuss is over. The case is closed. Dog goes missing. Ransom note is sent. Dog turns up. As far as the public and the press and for that matter the police are concerned, the kidnappers got cold feet and set the animal loose. There's no stolen property to be recovered and everybody can relax.'

'Precisely,' said Bognor. 'So that if Handyside had arranged the kidnapping himself so that he could collect the insurance, and if he then had second thoughts because he felt the police or the insurance company were getting suspicious, then this would be an obvious solution.'

'Much simpler,' said the Brigadier, 'to take the real dog back.'

'But suppose the real dog wasn't available. Suppose it had already been disposed of.'

The Brigadier looked at him sharply. 'Disposed of?' he echoed. But before he could enquire further there was a knock at the door and a minion appeared to say that the press wanted to ask questions about how the dog came to be in the Home.

'Keep all this to yourself,' he said, 'or at least check with me before using it. It could be highly embarrassing for everyone, not least the Home itself.' Bognor nodded.

The journalists' questions were routine, bored, almost perfunctory, and soon over. Afterwards Handyside walked across the room to Bognor.

'Satisfied?' he asked, eyes narrowed and mouth fixed in a smug smile.

'Not particularly,' said Bognor, 'but I'm glad you've got your dog back. If it really is your dog. I hear you were posting a dog to Copenhagen yesterday. A bull-dog, too?'

'What of it? I told you myself that I'd been to Heathrow. I picked the animal up from a client in Windsor. Everything was perfectly in order. You can check.'

'I already have,' said Bognor. He gazed at the bull-dog which was now in the process of being led away by one of the girls in swimwear. 'That dog,' he said, musingly, 'doesn't look as perky as it does in the advertisements. And if I didn't know better I'd say his coat looked a shade lack-lustre. A bit blurred at the edges.'

Handyside didn't move a muscle.

'Well, goodbye, Mr Bognor,' he said after a brief silence, 'I don't imagine we'll be meeting again. Unless you propose taking up dogs as a hobby. I presume your professional enquiries are at an end.'

'On the contrary,' he replied, 'they're only just beginning.'

Outside he decided that the Brigadier's revelation made a taxi a justifiable expense. He flagged one down on the hill and was back at the Board of Trade in half an hour.

'I really must go to Copenhagen. Now,' he said to Parkinson as soon as he was inside his superior's subterranean headquarters. 'I've solved it. If I can get hold of the real Raffles then I'm home and dry. And I'm virtually certain that the real Raffles is alive and well in Denmark. That Percy Pocklington is supervising his sale, using a reputable Danish breeder as a front man. Handyside dyed the real Raffles black. Now he's in Denmark he's been undyed and in the meantime they've got hold of some ordinary bulldog and painted him up to look like Raffles and he's the dog I saw at Richmond.'

'Steady on,' said Parkinson, who had been on the point of leaving for lunch and was greatly surprised by his subordinate's unheralded and exuberant arrival. 'Would you please start at the beginning and continue in chronological form until you come to the end. Then perhaps I shall understand.'

After ten minutes it was clear that Parkinson was as confused as Bognor had become. He picked up the phone and dialled his club. 'Parkinson here,' he said. 'Please tell Sir Charles I've been unavoidably detained and that I'll be with him as soon as I can.' Bognor appreciated the one-upmanship. 'Now,' Parkinson returned to the matter in hand. 'You want to go to Denmark to find the real Raffles?'

'Yes.'

'And your Kennel Club friends promise that he's there?'

'Yes.'

'And Brigadier Willoughby, whom I remember incidentally as a pompous pedant, claims that the Raffles here is merely some heavily camouflaged substitute?'

'Yes.'

'And if you succeed in capturing the real Raffles?'

'I'll bring him back here and confront them.'

Parkinson scribbled on his blotter. It looked from

where Bognor sat as if he was putting headings under a
plus and a minus but eventually he gave up.

'Oh, all right,' said his boss, flinging his pencil down
on the top of the desk. 'It can't do any more harm than
you've done already. Just remember that anything re-
motely controversial has to be done by the Danish
authorities. Not you. Not you at any price. I'll tell
them you're coming. Make your own arrangements
and stay no more than one night. The budget won't
stand it.'

'Mean sod,' thought Bognor as Parkinson left for
lunch in an ostentatious flurry of documents and paper.
He returned to his own room to contact Watherspoon.

By 3.30 he was airborne. He rather prided himself on
the speed of the operation, though certain formalities
could be curtailed when one was travelling on government business. The nonsense about checking in hours
before take-off was dispensed with altogether. It was
made easier by the fact that he only had one case, a
small black leather job, specifically designed for fitting
under aeroplane seats. Not that it often did, since the
undersides of aeroplane seats never conformed, but the
square tag on the case which said that it complied with
regulations meant that he could always take it as hand
baggage.

Watherspoon, too, had done his work admirably.
When Bognor first spoke to him he promised to telephone Copenhagen and make the necessary arrangements with Jorgen Winterfeld. By the time Bognor
reached the airport they had already been made. When
he rang a second time from the departure lounge
Watherspoon was able to tell him that Winterfeld would
meet him in the bar of the Hotel King Frederick in
Vester Voldgade at about six. Better still, he would
book a room for him in the same hotel. Winterfeld
would be reading a copy of the *Berlinske Tidende,* on
condition that Bognor carried the *Financial Times.* He
hoped to entertain Bognor to dinner.

He was almost contented as the plane settled down

to cruise above the cloud line. So much so that he ordered a quarter bottle of champagne. The events of the last few days receded along with the English coast and he amused himself by studying the legs of the air hostesses.

By the time they began their descent to Kastrup airport he had become sufficiently detached to run over a few salient features of the case so far. It was, he conceded, a muddle. So far he'd had two human deaths, one of which was more or less accidental and the other of which could not be proved to have anything to do with the smuggling ring. He didn't believe that Rose had been murdered by a passing maniac—well, not a maniac who just happened to be passing—but he knew he would have a job proving it. As well as these two he had a rabid dog, assuming medical reports on the Duchess's dog proved positive, and another of which the cause of death could not now be proved. He also had a kidnapped dog and a suspected case of substitution at the Dog-lovers' League Show. Mixed up with all this there was a great deal of subterfuge and clandestine goings-on, much of which he suspected was done merely to cloud the issue. He had a very definite feeling that people like Coriander and the Duchess, as well as Pocklington and Handyside, rather enjoyed subterfuge and deception for their own sakes. Furthermore he had a still firmer impression that one or two of them, most particularly Coriander, enjoyed confusing him not for any ulterior motive but simply because she enjoyed seeing him confused. And he was still confused. Of that, there was, alas, no question. He recognized too that if ever he were able to locate the real Raffles, not all would be solved. First of all he would have to prove that it was Raffles. That wouldn't be too difficult, but how to prove that it was the dog Handyside had shipped out on Sunday? He was still, he realized glumly, in the realms of speculation. Another bottle of champagne would have been pleasant but instead he merely tightened his seat belt and looked out of the window at the grey Danish sea coming up towards him.

After disembarking he travelled for an apparently interminable distance along a horizontal escalator before finding a taxi to the town centre. This was further than he had realized and the regular 'tick tick' of the meter clocking up yet more kroner made him uneasy. He had only brought £25 and his credit cards. He hoped it would be enough.

The King Frederick was near the town hall, opposite a large square, thronged with people and buses, and alongside the burnt-out remains of the Hotel Hafnia. It seemed comfortable enough and reminded Bognor vaguely of the old Mitre in the Oxford of his undergraduate days. He thought vaguely of checking in but instead went straight into the bar, which was dark, panelled and full of middle-aged men reading the *Berlinske Tidende*. Self-consciously he thrust his pink London paper under his elbow and stood still in the centre of the room. After a few seconds one of the newspaper readers, an immaculate individual with thinning grey hair and a pearl grey suit to match, stood up and advanced on him.

'Doctor Bognor, I presume,' he said, apparently seriously. 'I'm Jorgen Winterfeld. Welcome to Copenhagen. I hope you have had an excellent flight and the weather was good. Would you like to go to your room to freshen up or can I get you a drink?'

Mr Winterfeld's English, though stilted, was as immaculate as his appearance. Bognor said he'd like to have a drink before he freshened up and Mr Winterfeld suggested a 'gin-tonic'. Bognor agreed and the two of them sat down at a table.

'I hope you like fish,' said Mr Winterfeld. 'I find that many of my English friends are extremely charmed by our excellent fish. It is quite a speciality of ours in Copenhagen. I say it myself, I know, but they are usually doing it very well in this restaurant I shall take you to. As you say in England, it is done to a turn.'

Bognor said he liked fish.

'*Prosit* . . . cheers . . . *skol,*' said Mr Winterfeld hitting his glass against the side of Bognor's. 'This is your first visit to our beautiful city?'

Bognor agreed. Over the first drink they discussed generalities. Then Bognor went to his room, bathed and changed. Downstairs they had another drink, though Mr Winterfeld had obviously used the interval to have several more. The talk turned inevitably to blue movies of which Mr Winterfeld, slightly to Bognor's regret, professed a vehement disapproval. He considered that the pornographers had given clean living Danes like himself a bad name, and that Lord Longford had made himself and the country ridiculous. Not, of course, that he was opposed to sex, but . . .

It was not until they had arrived in the restaurant that Bognor was able to start on the subject of dogs. The restaurant was by the side of a narrow cobbled street overlooking a canal and above its entrance a simple neon light signalled the message: '*Fisk*'. It was indeed a *fisk* restaurant of an immediately recognizable style. Plain white table cloths, plain wooden chairs and plain matrons in black with white aprons. Bognor ordered a fish soup followed by eels and boiled potatoes. Mr Winterfeld asked for the soup and a whole sole, to be preceded by a litre of beer each and a glass of Aquavit.

'You've seen the dog?' said Bognor, tentatively.

'Ah yes, the famous dog. I have seen it,' said Mr Winterfeld portentously. 'Mr Larssen has asked for five thousand pounds of English money to be paid to a bank in Switzerland. It was this which made me suspicious.'

'Do you remember the name of the bank?'

'No. It was a very long name. I am more interested in the dog.'

'And you're sure the dog is Raffles?'

'Oh yes.' Mr Winterfeld looked serious. 'There is no doubting. You will see for yourself. I have arranged for Larssen to meet with my associates tomorrow in the city. He will have the dog with him. Then you shall judge.'

The soup arrived, thick with crustaceans, redolent of fennel.

'What sort of man is Larssen?'

Winterfeld slurped soup from his spoon, tore a segment from his bread roll and said, 'He is a weak man. As you English say, he is easily led. He knows a little about dogs and he travels sometimes to England. He breeds, how shall we say, satisfactorily. But he is not a great breeder.'

'So there is no question of this bulldog being his own production?'

'None at all. He makes very little pretence of it. He is acting as agent.'

'For Percy Pocklington?'

'I would imagine. But tomorrow you will see. Do you like the soup? It is a Danish speciality.'

Conversation now drifted away from things canine and Bognor allowed himself to enjoy his meal. It was, in an entirely simple and unpretentious way, an excellent meal. By the time they'd finished Bognor was replete and exhausted.

'I think, if you'll forgive me,' he said, 'I'll go to bed fairly early.'

'But of course,' said Mr Winterfeld. 'But it is not far to walk and if we make a little detour I will show you Stroget. You have heard of Stroget?'

'No. I am afraid not.'

'It is our famous walking street where there is no traffic. It has many of the finest shops in all Copenhagen; there is glass and furniture and porcelain. It is like your own Bond Street in London, although sadly it is being spoilt with many vulgar novelties. Even in Stroget there are "Live Shows" and "Porno Shops". It is too bad. In a few years I think there will be no Stroget like today. It will be more like your Soho than Bond Street.' He laughed sourly.

Outside it was crisp and a light breeze cut up from the canal making Bognor's eyes water. It was dark here, though the stars were bright, but within a few minutes they were at the end of the Stroget, where there was enough neon to see clearly. They walked slowly, stopping every few yards for Mr Winterfeld to point out the delights of the Royal Danish Porcelain shop, or Illums Bolighus. Occasionally a more garish shop front would appear under the sign 'PORNO' and Bognor would have a fleeting glimpse of trusses and dildos and magazines portraying naked sex of every description. Mr Winterfeld hurried past these shops averting his eyes.

Half-way up the street, Bognor saw a cinema showing *Deep Throat,* the American blue movie which had, amidst much publicity, been banned from Britain. As they drew alongside Mr Winterfeld once more quickened his pace, though Bognor tried to linger and stare, not altogether idly, at the pictures of Linda Lovelace outside the place. He was trying to look censorious rather than prurient when the swing doors of the cinema opened and out came an over-dapper figure with a spivlike moustache and a dark blue, velvet-collared overcoat. For a second Bognor stared at the man, then swiftly looked away and hurried after Winterfeld.

'Quick,' he said, 'let's hide. I've just seen Percy Pocklington.'

Mr Winterfeld reacted swiftly. They were just passing a bar, and without further prompting he stepped inside followed by Bognor. Only after he had ordered two brandies did he say anything.

'Where was he?'

'Coming out of the cinema. The one showing *Deep Throat.*'

Mr Winterfeld made a face. 'I have often supposed that he was that sort of person. Did he see you?'

'I don't know.'

Mr Winterfeld sighed. 'It would be unfortunate if he did see you. It might put him on the alert. But it is unlikely. He will have been preoccupied.'

Bognor wondered if Percy Pocklington's eyes had indeed been blinded by lust and decided, regretfully, that sex-crazed though he might have been, he was not the sort of man to miss him.

'I have a nasty feeling he saw me,' he said, 'and that he recognized me. And that he will have realized why I'm here.'

'Courage, Mr. Bognor,' said Winterfeld. 'Let us hope you are mistaken.'

Next morning Mr Winterfeld sent a large white Mercedes to the King Frederick, and in this Bognor was conveyed to an office in Hans Christian Andersen's Boulevard. The journey took three minutes and covered no more than a few hundred yards. Mr Winterfeld was clearly trying to impress. Or perhaps he was paving the way for disappointment.

His host was waiting for him at the entrance to the office block, as affable and impeccable as he'd been the night before.

'Larssen and the dog are due here at ten o'clock,' he said. 'We have coffee now and you shall meet my colleagues.'

Upstairs the colleagues, presumably (though it was not made entirely clear) the directors or senior management of the advertising agency, were gathered together round an oval table. A small stage was brightly lit and under the focus of a television camera. Two closed-circuit receivers hung from the ceiling.

'We intend putting Raffles—or whoever he may be—through his paces,' said Mr Winterfeld, introducing the men, all similarly in anonymous grey, in a mixture of Danish and English. They all creased into instant smiles of greeting only to relapse into a gloomy discussion in their native language.

'If we are all satisfied that the dog is Raffles we have a problem,' said Mr Winterfeld. 'What I suggest is that we pay the money required by Mr Larssen and retain the dog for tests to be made. It is always possible to stop the cheque.'

'If you think he'll agree to relinquish the dog.'

'Oh yes. There will be no choice.' Winterfeld seemed adamant and Bognor, still unsure, drank his coffee in silence. Winterfeld went to speak to one of the Danes and left Bognor to ponder. The others seemed to have accepted his presence among them with surprising equanimity. He had no idea how Winterfeld had explained him. There was an ultra-modern digital clock with four faces on the middle of the boardroom table, and it showed 9.55. He tried not to let it mesmerize him but he was beginning to have doubts about the materialization of the Excelsior Chewing Gum Dog.

At ten o'clock the others began to look expectant. A technician tested the camera while one of the executives stood on the stage smiling self-consciously. It seemed to work. At five past the expectancy had become nervous. Feet were being shuffled, papers riffled, cigarettes smoked with a hint of exasperation. At ten past the irritation was palpable and unmistakable. Still no sign of Larssen and the dog. After another five minutes the senior man spoke to Winterfeld peremptorily, pointing several times to his watch. Winterfeld shrugged helplessly and picked up the phone on the table, waited and asked for a number. Bognor picked out the word 'Odense' in his request and assumed that he was ringing Larssen's home.

Everybody was watching him now. Eventually he started to talk to someone, very politely at first, then in shorter and shorter sentences until with a crisp expletive, he smashed the receiver down.

'He must have seen you last night,' he said to Bognor. 'That was Mrs Larssen. She says her husband went away at dawn taking the dog with him. She had no idea where he was going, but she says he was very agitated last night when there was a phone call. He has changed all his plans.'

He turned back to his colleagues and splayed his

arms in a gesture of frustrated impotence. There followed a fairly acid exchange in Danish which ended in the disintegration of the meeting.

'So,' said Winterfeld, gathering up paper and stuffing it into a briefcase, 'your dog has flown. It will be impossible to find now.'

'I can ask the police,' said Bognor, desperately.

'They're too busy catching criminals,' said Winterfeld, 'they will not be interested in a dog. Besides the dog has probably fled abroad already. I am sorry.'

'Oh bloody hell,' said Bognor. 'It must have been that little creep Pocklington. He must have seen me last night and tipped Larssen off. You're perfectly right. We'll never catch them now. With their capacity for disguise and subterfuge they'd have turned the bulldog into a Chesapeake Bay or a Belgian waffle hound by now and it'll turn up in some dog show in Ankara or Addis.'

'The Emperor Haile Selassie has some remarkable bulldogs,' said Mr Winterfeld. 'You may be right.'

They were out in the street now, and it had turned cold. Bognor hunched his shoulders against the chill breeze.

'And now,' asked Mr Winterfeld, 'what will you do now?'

Bognor looked blankly at the pavement. 'I suppose,' he said, 'I have no alternative but to go back to my office and admit to failure. Then start all over again. I have the impression they may be rattled.'

Mr Winterfeld raised his eyebrows. '*Au contraire,*' he said, 'it is my opinion that your enemies are in danger of over-optimism. They may over-reach themselves. It is perhaps best for you to return empty-handed. As you say in England "it may mull them into a sense of false security". However, I must go now. Can you arrange your return? The car will take you to the hotel and they will be sure to make the necessary bookings. There are usually empty places on the flights to London.'

They shook hands and Bognor returned in the Mercedes utterly dejected. Once more the trail had gone cold and he had no idea how to continue. The thought of Parkinson's reaction appalled him.

He picked up his bags at the King Frederick and asked the hall porter to book him on a flight home. While he waited he read the *Herald Tribune* and watched the gentle ebb and flow of international business executives in and out of the lobby. He was reflecting on the uniformity of this class of person when another hall porter called over to him.

'Mr Bognor?'

'Yes.'

'There is a parcel.'

'Parcel?'

Bognor walked over to the desk and the man produced a very small oblong package wrapped in brown paper. It was addressed quite distinctly and neatly in block capital letters to 'S. Bognor, Esq., King Frederick Hotel'. The lettering was in biro and Bognor knew enough about forensic science to realize that it would be impossible to detect its origins. He took the parcel back to his chair and unwrapped it. Inside there was a packet of Excelsior Chewing Gum and a note on Basildon Bond writing paper. It was written in the same anonymous biro capitals and said, 'Chew over this and think of wafers made with honey.' He sat and stared at it for a few moments, turned it over, held it up to the light, thus confirming that it was indeed Basildon Bond, and couldn't work it out. Handyside's ransom note had been written on Basildon Bond but it was one of the most common writing papers in Britain. That proved nothing. Almost without thinking he extracted one of the slivers of gum from the gaudy red and yellow packet and began to obey the instructions by chewing. It didn't taste in the least like honey and it had none of the consistency of a wafer. Like other chewing gum it was simply soggy mint. He was so engrossed in his mastication and rumination that he failed to notice the desk clerk's further calls. Eventually he realized that a flight had been arranged and a taxi for the airport was outside. Reluctantly he picked up his luggage, thanked and tipped the clerk and left. All the way back to London he thought about honey and wafers and Basildon Bond, but it meant less and less the more he chewed. The only undeniable fact was that his antagonists were becoming, as Winterfeld had suggested, dangerously cocky. The chewing gum and its cryptic accompaniment were a tease, and if the gang was teasing him then, given a little more rope, it might well hang. Alas, for Bognor, he was well aware that Parkinson was most unlikely to allow more rope. He would feel that too much had been given already.

As usual, Bognor's predictions regarding Parkinson were sadly accurate. His boss listened in silence to his tale of frustration and woe, then commented, 'So all you have to show for your jaunt is a packet of chewing gum and a meaningless message?'

'I saw Pocklington.'

'But we all knew Pocklington was going to be there. He had a perfectly good reason for being there. It's scarcely surprising that you saw him.'

'He must have told Larssen.'

'Speculation.'

'The dog *was* there.'

'Conjecture.'

'Winterfeld's an expert. He saw the animal.'

'So you say. I'm not impressed. In fact if I were to be frank I'm appalled, aghast, amazed, apoplectic with anger.'

All this he said with the icy self-control which Bognor knew he adopted only when he was very very cross indeed.

'I'm sorry,' said Bognor, defeated, 'I really did think I was getting somewhere.'

'But, alas, you were mistaken,' said Parkinson, still frigid. 'You have gone round in the proverbial circle. As usual you've accumulated a wealth of tittle-tattle and gossip and innuendo and scarcely a single fact. Can you imagine the sort of case we would present in court? We'd be a laughing stock.'

Bognor was silent. He realized, forlornly, that there was nothing to say. He had failed again.

'As I see it,' said Parkinson, who appeared to realize that further fury was superfluous, 'there is one goal you have achieved.'

Bognor brightened momentarily, then remembered just in time that Parkinson's faint compliments always preceded some crushingly climactic insult.

'Your friend Winterfeld,' he continued, 'suggested that our smugglers were becoming over-confident. He's quite possibly correct. I am prepared to concede that your present of chewing gum could be in some oblique way related to the matter in hand. And if they have been provoked into sending such childish messages then they can only have been provoked into it by your staggering display of stupefying incompetence.'

Bognor, staring at Her Majesty the Queen on the wall behind him, blinked hard and focused on the regal tiara. He was hurt by Parkinson's remarks but he knew better than to show it. He said nothing.

'You had better,' Parkinson went on, 'return to your beginnings, since that is where your eccentric travels have deposited you in any case. I suggest you go back to the Kennel Club and to Mr Watherspoon and to the Duchess of Dorset and to Mrs Potts and to all the other improbable characters upon whom you have stumbled. Perhaps then you may find something worthy of the name of evidence. But please, no more gallivanting. Just try to employ some self-discipline.'

For days Bognor made lists and programmes, tearing them up as soon as he had compiled them. He met Watherspoon for a cup of coffee and the man commiserated but could offer no further help. He discussed it all with Monica but she was more interested in the gallery. He purchased dog dictionaries and dog encyclopaedias and dog magazines and newspapers and scoured their pages in a vain search for evidence. He contemplated re-interviewing the Duchess and Handy-side and Coriander Cordingley and Pocklington but could think of no way in which he could extract the information he required.

The inquest on Rose, Ailsa Potts' kennelmaid, was adjourned but the police persisted in their view that her killing was the work of a Surblington Strangler, and were abetted in this view by the press who printed lurid stories about the 'wild beast who still roams the leafy lanes'.

It was confirmed that there was an outbreak of rabies at the Duchess's, but comment was largely flippant and it was generally assumed that the disease had been caused by some mysterious freak of circumstances which was better left uninvestigated. Parkinson began by asking Bognor about his progress but soon desisted, and eventually even Bognor became listless and apathetic. He began to believe that the assignment would be allowed to drag on indefinitely, never requiring a solution but, supposedly, keeping him occupied and out of harm's way. In his most extreme moments of introspective gloom he even wondered if the entire episode had not been dreamt up by another department of the Board of Trade solely for his benefit. As the days dragged by this last idea became more deeply lodged in his mind and he found that he spent hours on end sitting at his desk surrounded by a protective screen of canine publications while actually engaged in an uphill struggle with *The Times* crossword.

Then, a week after his unhappy return from Denmark, he had a second break, and this time it seemed certain to be a winner. He had just decided that '13 down—College building mortgaged to pay Paul (10)' must be Peterhouse, when his phone went and the main door announced that a Mr Ramble was there to see him.

8

Albert Ramble was agitated. His strong unflappable face was mobile with anxiety and his tie was awry. When he shook hands with Bognor his grasp seemed almost peremptory and his greeting was disjointed.

'I came at once,' he said. 'Felt you would know what to do.'

'Let's find somewhere to talk,' said Bognor. 'It's not very discreet here. Nor exactly comfortable.'

It was 12.30, and for a moment he thought of suggesting the Italian café, but thought better of it. He hadn't been back since Rose was killed and he doubted whether he would. A return meal would somehow be lacking in respect. In the case of Mr Ramble he decided a pub would be more appropriate. He suggested the Perch and Parrot and Mr Ramble agreed. His trousers were specked with dog hairs and his own locks were uncharacteristically dishevelled. As they were about to leave the building Parkinson passed them, walking purposefully. He glanced at the two men, raised his eyebrows, seemed on the point of speech, but instead strode on.

In the pub Mr Ramble asked diffidently if he could have a Scotch, which again, Bognor guessed, was uncharacteristic. They sat down in a corner as quiet as they could find. It was still noisy and convivial but their fellow drinkers were engrossed in their small talk and their secretaries. It was as safe a place as any.

'This came in the first post,' said Mr Ramble, taking

145

the whisky like medicine. He pulled a piece of pale blue paper, folded in two, from his inside breast pocket. To Bognor it was instantly familiar.

'Basildon Bond, I see,' he said, knowledgeably.

Mr Ramble glanced at him with amused surprise. 'As a matter of fact, yes,' he said. 'I use it myself somtimes. It's not exactly rare, is it?'

'I suppose not.' Bognor felt deflated again. For a moment he'd been almost pleased. Mr Ramble handed him the paper. There were several sentences on it, picked out in letters torn from newspapers. The style was the same as in Mr Handyside's ransom note, though Bognor had the sinking feeling that he couldn't prove it even if the ransom note still existed. And he was nearly certain that by now the letter would have been destroyed. The lettering was expertly laid out. 'We, a highly exclusive agency, are prepared to arrange showing of your Perfect Prettyboy in important foreign shows waiving all quarantine restrictions. Complete confidence guaranteed. Foreign stud fees virtually certain if required. Fees negotiable on percentage of commission basis. Reply to . . .' There followed an address in Tottenham. Bognor read it and re-read it.

'Who's Perfect Prettyboy?' he asked.

'Toy poodle,' said Mr Ramble. 'I've been keeping very quiet about him so far but he's the best I've ever done. No question. Actually it's a bit of a fluke but he's near perfect. Only seven inches high but strong with it. Marvellous temperament, well muscled loins, plenty of spring, carries himself beautifully. But he's still young and I want to bring him on slow. Heaven knows how this lot found out about him. As I say I've been keeping quiet about the little boy. He'd have been one in the eye for Ailsa Potts, though she does concentrate on standards. I tell you,' he finished his drink, 'unless we're lumbered with biased judges like Pocklington he'll win everything.'

'My impression,' said Bognor, 'is that if you go along with this you'll have a biased judge exactly like Pocklington, with the considerable advantage that he'll be on your side.'

'I suppose so,' Mr Ramble sighed. 'So what do you suggest I do?' he asked.

'You must play along with them,' said Bognor eagerly. 'Answer the letter, telling them you'd love to let them show Perfect Prettyboy abroad. When they reply you do what they ask, exactly as if you were really falling in with their scheme. Keep me informed of every development and leave the rest to me.'

Mr Ramble pursed his lips and looked doubtful.

'Can't you trace the letter? Have it analysed or something? And the address. Surely if you go there and confront them you've done it all.'

Bognor smiled, rather as Parkinson might when confronted by his own innocence. 'I'll have it analysed, of course,' he said, 'but I can't hold out much hope. Basildon Bond is very common, as you yourself point out. The letters are cut from newspapers and are therefore untraceable. There might be fingerprints, but I'll wager there aren't, and I'll be very surprised if we're dealing with people who have criminal records.'

'The address then?' Mr Ramble was very obviously reluctant to agree with Bognor.

'You may be right,' said Bognor, 'but it's almost bound to be an accommodation address. A staging post. I'll investigate it but I don't hold out much hope. Easily our best chance of success is to follow this through and catch the smugglers *in flagrante*.'

'How?'

'Aha,' said Bognor, beginning, for the first time in ages, to feel confidence returning. 'I shall follow your dog until it is on the point of being illegally removed from the country and at that precise moment I shall, as it were, blow the whistle.'

Mr Ramble was still more doubtful. Bognor went to the bar for more drinks and came back with them and ham sandwiches besides.

'One aspect worries me,' he said, eyebrows beetling with concern. 'Would you be able to identify your dog?'

'I'd recognize him. Straight away. No problem.'

'That wasn't what I asked,' said Bognor, almost brusque with buoyancy. 'It's no good recognizing him. You have to prove that you recognize him. Even with Raffles, for instance, there was no way of proving incontrovertibly that the dog *was* Raffles, or not, as the case may be.'

'Name disc,' said Ramble, speculatively.

'Hardly. Easily removed. What about tattooing?'

'Possible,' he said. 'Don't like it though. You can damage a dog tattooing it. Hepatitis if there's anything wrong with the needles. Besides, if you use a vibrator they can't stand the noise. Not if they're more than ten weeks old.'

'Must you use a vibrator?'

'Could use a clamp. Don't like it though.'

'Why not?'

'I just don't hold with it.'

'It seems to me that it's essential,' said Bognor. 'You have to be able to say with absolute certainty that will stand up in a court of law that the dog is yours.'

Mr Ramble peeled some bread off a ham sandwich, peered at it disparagingly, replaced it and put the sandwich in his mouth.

'I still don't like it,' he said.

'Why not?'

'Suppose something goes wrong?'

'Nothing can go wrong. It's out of the question. Now you must write back at once. Send a postcard. Just say, um, "Accept kind offer. Please advise terms, arrangements, etc." Then sit back and await developments.'

'Hmmm,' Mr Ramble sat hunched over his sandwiches and alcohol, exuding disappointment. He had obviously hoped for a speedy solution but now found himself inextricably embroiled. Bognor took pity on him.

'I promise I'll have the letter analysed and the address checked before I ask you to do more. If I'm correct will you promise to help along the lines I've suggested?'

'I suppose so.' He was almost surly now. Bognor was surprised.

'Come, Mr Ramble,' he said. 'Think of your obligations to dogdom. You owe it to your friends and colleagues. They'll be eternally in your debt.'

'I doubt it,' he said. 'If you ask me they're all in it except me. All bent. If I help put the dog smugglers behind bars I'll be ostracized.'

'In the doghouse, in fact,' said Bognor, and wished he hadn't. 'Seriously though. Think of Mrs Protheroe. There must be others like her.'

'I doubt it,' he said, standing up, 'but I'll do what I can all the same. I've let myself in for it and I'll see it through if it's the last thing I do.'

'I'm sure it won't be,' said Bognor. 'I'll keep your letter if I may. For analysis. Don't do anything until I call you.'

As soon as he got back to the office he sent the letter to the laboratory. It was received with superciliousness, but it was at least received. He had feared that after his last offering, the cake tin of bonfire ashes, he would be turned away. Then, true to his word, he took the tube to Tottenham.

The address was almost precisely what he had expected—a dingy corner newsagent's with cards outside advertising 'French lessons', 'Strict schoolmistresses' and second-hand mopeds and perambulators. Outside on the dusty pavement half a dozen children played football and an old man in a tweed overcoat that had once, many years ago, been almost respectable, leaned against a hoarding and stared unseeing at the slow moving traffic.

Bognor pushed the door open and it swung back with a clang from the bell. An elderly woman wearing a headscarf looked up from the nudie magazine, open at the gatefold, which she was perusing. More soft porn lay round her on the counter in among *Practical Roller-skating, Homes and Gardens* and *Woman's Realm*.

'Afternoon,' he said, feeling that civility might yield

results. The woman looked at him expressionlessly, a smouldering cigarette hanging limply from the corner of her mouth. Civility, he realized, pained, was going to have no effect.

'Box 301,' he said. 'Could you give me the name and address of the user?'

'What?' said the shopkeeper, removing the cigarette grudgingly.

'Name and address of the owner of Box 301.'

'It's confidential.'

'I'm official.' He produced his card and flashed it under her resentful eyes. It might have been a Diner's Club card for all the effect it produced.

'You can piss off,' she said, replacing the cigarette.

'I most certainly will not piss off,' he said. 'You tell me who has that box number or I'll get the police round.' He was damned if he was going to be sworn at by some porn-peddling grandmother in North London.

'You piss off and get the bleeding police,' she said. 'See if I care.'

Normally he wouldn't have bothered, but today he was feeling uncharacteristically aggressive. He slammed the door, almost fell over one of the tiny footballers and hurried off in search of the nearest police station. It was close by in the main street and the occupants were perfectly civil. The duty officer identified the newsagent's, said it was probably Mavis, and deputed a young constable to go back with him. He couldn't tell whether such service was the result of his Board of Trade Identity Card, or the fact that they were having a slack afternoon.

Mavis was still sullen when they returned. She and the constable were evidently acquainted.

'You'll have to tell the gentleman,' said the policeman. He was bored, matter-of-fact, but he sounded and looked authoritative.

'Can't tell what I don't know,' grumbled the old girl.

'What do you mean?' asked Bognor.

'Never the same bloke,' she said. 'Don't know their

names. Never know when they're coming. They take all the three hundreds.'

Bognor raised his eyebrows and the constable nodded. 'That's usual, sir,' he said. 'Whoever your man is, he won't pick up himself. He'll use a delivery service. Makes it just that bit more foolproof.'

'Does he—do they—come in at a regular time?'

'No. Could be any time, any day. After hours sometimes. No telling when they'll be in.'

Both she and the policeman obviously reckoned they'd done enough. Bognor sighed. There was not much point in pursuing it. He could wait for the collector and follow him round, but he had better ideas. His only reason for coming to Tottenham was his sense of obligation to Albert Ramble. Like the others he'd probably done enough. He thanked them and returned to the station.

On his desk when he returned was a buff envelope with the elaborate insignia Whitehall gave to anything urgent and confidential. It was Albert Ramble's letter together with the analyst's report. 'Basildon Bond writing paper,' it said. 'Letters cut from *Times* and *Daily Mail*. No prints.' He smiled. It wasn't proof but it suggested probability. After all it was unlikely that there were two independent groups operating in the dog world and sending out curious anonymous letters cut from *The Times* and the *Mail* and pasted on Basildon Bond.

He telephoned to Ramble and told him of the afternoon's development. Ramble listened in silence.

'I'm sorry,' said Bognor. 'I've done what I could.'

'I see that,' said Ramble. 'I'm sorry too.'

'Will you write to them?'

'I suppose I have to.'

'Just say, "Delighted, accept kind suggestion, please supply further details". Something like that. How long will it take to get the dog tattooed?'

'My vet will have a clip. I can do it tonight if you think it's wise.'

'It could be as well. I expect they move fast once they get a go-ahead.'

'All right.'

'Just let me know as soon as anything happens.'

'Yes.'

Then he telephoned Watherspoon of the Kennel Club, and asked him to find out what shows Percy Pocklington was judging during the next month. Watherspoon asked no questions and promised to reply in the morning. When he'd replaced the receiver Bognor sat for several minutes sucking the end of his pencil. Then he decided against making a list. It was uncommonly careless of them to approach such a pillar of honesty as Ramble but presumably it was always a risk. Besides it was unlikely that anyone else would do what Ramble had done. Much more likely to throw the letter away and pretend it had never happened. He wondered if that was what Mrs Potts had done. If the old fatty had refused to deal with them it was at least conceivable that they'd tried to twist her arm, and that as the threats had increased so they'd finally had a bluff called and been compelled to kill her prize poodle. Since Bognor was convinced that there was a psychopath involved he felt that was a probable answer.

He wondered if he should tell Parkinson now, but guessed that his superior would categorize his scheme as 'gallivanting', calculated to bring the Board and Department into disrepute. He would leave it as long as he could and present Parkinson with a *fait accompli* —well, nearly *accompli*.

That night he told Monica his scheme over dinner at the Barque and Bite, a floating restaurant on the canal past the zoo. It was close enough to walk to and they enjoyed the gentle though occasional undulations of the deck beneath them and the shriek of some exotic bird or animal which sometimes punctuated the meal.

'Awfully dangerous,' said Monica, sipping sherry and fiddling with a bowl of nuts.

'Why?'

'You were hit on the head in the Duchess's park.

Rose has been murdered, they've done a remarkable sleight of hand with the chewing gum dog, Mr Sparks has died mysteriously of acquired rabies. Whately Wonderful was murdered as well. They've made a perfect fool of you wherever you've been and you ask why I think it's dangerous. Honestly.'

'My theory is that they've been lulled . . .'

'Into a sense of false security,' she chorused. 'I know. It's always your theory when you've ballsed things up. But this time I think you're being ridiculous. There's a whole gang of them and only one of you, and they're extremely accomplished and ruthless and you're, well . . .' She put out a hand to touch his and smiled sweetly but patronizingly. 'Well, you aren't really cut out for this sort of thing, are you? Really?'

Bognor bridled. The waiter brought palm hearts for two.

'I shall have a back-up squad. Police. All I'll do is to follow them until they commit an offence.'

'When's that?'

'The minute the dog leaves port or airport without an export licence.'

'Oh. Have you told Parkinson?'

'Not yet.'

'Shouldn't you?'

'I have a feeling that he'd veto it or take the operation over for himself.'

'I think he'd be right.'

They dropped the subject after that and alternated between discussion of the food and the art gallery. In the silences they listened to their neighbours who were gossiping dangerously about cabinet ministers. They evidently had privileged information.

There was no news from Albert Ramble next day, though Watherspoon rang to say that in a week's time Pocklington was off on another transatlantic jaunt. The next day produced nothing from Ramble either but oddly there was an invitation to drinks from Coriander Cordingley. It was for that same evening and he accepted. Later she rang again to say that something had cropped up and she'd had to cancel the party, which was, in any case, just a few friends. However she was going to be in the Westminster area. Why didn't they meet? Say the American bar at the Savoy? Again Bognor accepted.

'Haven't seen you for ages,' she said, arriving ten minutes late and ordering a dry martini. 'I'm beginning to be afraid you've lost interest in dogdom.'

'No,' said Bognor, aroused as before by her painted and scented and suggestively diaphanous appearance. 'Just stuck, that's all.'

'Can I help?'

'I don't know. Maybe. Have you heard anything suspicious?' he asked.

'Not so much as a whisper,' she simpered. 'It wouldn't surprise me if you've scared them off.'

'Who?'

'Your smugglers.'

'Yes, but who are they?' asked Bognor. 'You must have an idea. As you must have realized, I have my suspicions.'

'But you can't prove anything?'

'Not yet.'

'But whom do you suspect?'

'Everyone I've met.' He went through the list, then chancing his arm a little, told her the story of his trip to Copenhagen. He said nothing about his latest plan.

'What dreadful cheek,' she said, 'sending you chewing gum. That doesn't sound like Percy Pocklington. He doesn't have that much sense of humour. And the note? What did it say?'

'Something about wafers and honey.'

She frowned, puzzled. 'What exactly? What does it mean?'

'I really don't know,' he replied. 'Too cryptic for me. I don't think it's that important. Another drink?'

'No, thank you,' she said. 'I've got some sketches to do this evening. I'm late with them already. Have you made any contact with Mr Eagerly?'

'No. Why?'

'Oh,' she smiled again, tantalizingly. 'I just thought he was one of your original suspects. And if you suspect everybody . . . I think he's worth your time. Fascinating man. The Dog Centre's a wonderful place. Right away in the hills, tucked into a valley. Beautiful. You should go just for the experience.'

'Hmmm,' he said.

Later that night he got the call he'd been waiting for.

'I'm to have the dog ready tomorrow evening at eight sharp,' said Mr Ramble. 'They take 50 per cent of the first £1000, and 25 after that.'

'How did they contact you?'

'Telephone. It was a man.'

'Did you recognize the voice?'

'No. But it sounded disguised. He was talking with a sort of foreign, German accent. Not a very good one. He sounded muffled too, as though he was talking through a handkerchief.'

'And that was all he said?'

'Yes. He didn't take long.'

'O.K.,' said Bognor. 'Do as he says. Get the dog ready and I'll be with you tomorrow afternoon. How do I get there?'

Ramble gave the directions—a complex series of manoeuvres in the more rural parts of Hertfordshire —and Bognor promised to be there by five.

'Who was that?' asked Monica, afterwards.

'Ramble. My plan's going into operation.'

'Oh God.' Monica was plainly disturbed. 'What does Parkinson say?'

'He doesn't,' said Bognor. 'He won't even know until I call him from Ramble's kennels.' He watched Monica's face fall and gave her a comforting embrace. 'It'll be all right,' he said. 'He can't not support me at that stage.'

The Ramble kennels took some finding; they were at the end of a track leading nowhere, three miles out of the tiny village of Tuck Baldring, a small complex of sheds and huts clustered round a black and white timbered farmhouse. Bognor arrived just after five to find Ramble in a state of advanced neurosis.

'I don't like this,' he said, sitting over a strong coffee in the kitchen. 'Seems to me that I'm aiding and abetting a felony. In any case I'm likely to lose the dog and it's irreplaceable. I won't have another like him in my lifetime.'

Bognor tried to transmit a confidence he was far from feeling. What worried him even more than the impending escapade was the conversation with Parkinson in which he was going to have to reveal his deception.

'It'll be all right,' he said. 'Remember the dog's tattooed. He can't be stolen property. We're bound to get him back. America's law abiding.'

'Supposing he ends up in Brazil,' said Ramble bitterly. 'Can't even get bloody Ronald Biggs out of Brazil. Not much chance of getting poor old Prettyboy out.'

'They're not going to Brazil.'

'You don't know that.'

Bognor didn't, so he countered by saying that there was no reason for them to go to Brazil, and asked to see the dog. Ramble led him outside to a lean-to at the side of the house. Inside there were bales of straw, sacks of dogmeal, a collection of rusty oil drums and, on a heavy wooden work bench, a small wire cage with a leather handle attached to the top. Inside lay a small black bundle in tartan wrapping. The bundle moved rhythmically and emitted a sound uncannily like that of the human snore.

'There he is,' said Ramble unnecessarily. 'Poor little chap.'

'He's very small,' said Bognor, unable to think of anything more intelligent.

'Seven inches high,' said his owner, 'like I told you, but perfectly sound.'

They stared at him for a few moments and then went back into the house. Bognor asked to use the phone which was in the living room. This, like its owner, was very masculine and slightly worn at the edges. There was no sign of Mrs Protheroe's influence nor that of any other female, and the pervading atmosphere was one, not so much of dirt, as of mess.

'Progress?' asked Parkinson, when they'd made contact. 'Haven't seen you since you were in the hall with that dogged looking fellow the other day. He looked like something to do with dogs. Was he?'

'Yes, I'm with him now.'

'Doing what?'

Bognor told him, and was rewarded with a long, heavily charged silence.

'How long have you known all this?'

'Only since yesterday,' Bognor lied.

'I'm going to have words with you, my son,' said Parkinson, 'but not now. You've been your usual idiotic self, but your thinking is sound in one respect. It's too late to call you off. I'll do the necessary. Ring me the minute you have enough and I'll put an emergency call straight through to the nearest police. I'll alert Heathrow now. They seem most likely.'

'Thank you, sir.'

'You won't thank me by the time I've finished with you,' said Parkinson. 'All I ask now is that you don't attempt any more of your single-handed heroics. They scare me. Just watch and see who picks up the dog, then follow at a safe distance but for God's sake don't lose them. And, quite as important, don't let them see you.'

'Right.'

He hung up and went back into the kitchen, where Ramble was boiling the kettle for more coffee.

'I'll hide the car in the garage,' he said, 'and I'd better sit in it while they're here. I'll want to make a quick getaway if I'm not going to lose them.'

Ramble said nothing, just poured water into their mugs, which already contained heaped spoonfuls of powdered instant coffee.

'Is that all right?'

'I suppose so.'

They drank another half mug of coffee then went

outside again and squeezed the car into the garage alongside Ramble's elderly Land Rover. The door was wooden and there were cracks both in it and around it. He would be able to watch from there in safety. Indoors again they drank yet more coffee and listened to the radio. From time to time Ramble would stand up and move over to the window, peering out as if he were expecting his visitors early. Shortly after seven he announced that he was going to walk round to check that everything was as it should be. He would also bring Perfect Prettyboy into the kitchen ready for delivery.

'Best if you go and hide now, isn't it?' he asked nervously.

Bognor didn't much relish the thought of a whole hour alone in a draughty garage. There'd be bound to be rats and he had a horror of rodents which almost matched his dislike of dogs. Still, he recognized that it would be more tactful as well as safer to agree.

As he sat in the driving seat he wondered if it was going to be over and done with as easily as he hoped. The plan seemed almost too simple. It was quite light in the garage since there were not only cracks in and around the doors but between the corrugated iron roof and the walls, in the walls themselves and from around another small door at the back. Presently he got out of the Mini and found a good vantage point at the right of the door. From it he could see the yard and the whole area at the front of the house. He stood there for a moment, one eye screwed to the crack, then straightened and went back to the car. He'd filled up with petrol and checked the oil in the village. That meant he had enough for two hundred miles, which wouldn't be necessary if his quarry only went as far as Heathrow airport. His watch said 7.30. Half an hour to wait. He contemplated a cheroot and decided against it, then sat still and listened. Somewhere behind him there was, as he'd feared, a scuttling of small animals. He gritted his teeth and wondered what to expect.

The garage was cold and by the time the half hour

had elapsed he was shivering. It was still light outside but the sun had lost its warmth. He screwed his eye up to his viewing slit and waited. There wasn't a sound anywhere, and even the garage mice or rats were resting. He strained to listen for the sound of a car and then realized that straining was unnecessary. Any car coming down the lane would be for Ramble. It had to be. There was nowhere else.

At three minutes past eight the front door opened and Ramble came out, a glass in one hand. He stood for a moment sniffing the evening air, as nervous and apprehensive as Bognor, then turned and went back in. Five minutes later, Bognor heard the vehicle. It came slowly down the lane, turned carefully into the yard, sidelights on, and stopped immediately before the front door about thirty yards from Bognor's straining eye. It was still light enough to see that it was a van, and to make out the lettering on the side. Bognor sucked in his breath sharply in a mixture of triumph and excitement. The sign on the side said 'Animal Transport Ltd. Prop. C. Handyside'. A second later he sucked in his breath even more sharply when the door of the van opened and a trim figure in a trouser suit and costermonger's cap stepped out. It wasn't, as he'd expected, Cecil Handyside, but Coriander Cordingley. She walked purposefully to the front door, rang the bell and was instantly admitted. Bognor remained at his post. He had, of course, realized that Coriander was implicated, but somehow he had not expected her to be involved in quite this way. He had sensed that her artistry might have been instrumental in disguising Raffles and his counterfeit namesake. He had seen her conferring in the bright night of the Duchess of Dorset's park. He had, for heaven's sake, woken, innocent, in her bed. All the same, absurd though it might seem, he had not been expecting her; and he had hoped that when the time came for a heavy hand to be laid on a miscreant shoulder that the shoulder would be Handyside's or Pocklington's, or perhaps even the Duchess's.

'Blast,' he said.

She was inside for just over five minutes, then just as Bognor was becoming suspicious about the length of her stay, she bustled out of the house carrying the cage in her right hand. She went straight to the rear of the vehicle; opened the doors; deposited her prize, which still appeared to be asleep; slammed the doors to; waved gaily to Ramble who stood, fidgeting, in the porch; climbed into the driving seat, revved the engine and was away almost before Bognor realized what had happened. He stood for a moment watching the disappearing tail lights, then saw that Ramble was already hurrying towards the garage, and himself climbed into his car and switched on the ignition.

'Miss Cordingley, the painter,' said Ramble, breathlessly after he'd opened the garage.

'So I saw,' said Bognor. 'Did she say anything?'

'Nothing worth repeating. Mentioned something about the States, that was all. Nothing more specific than that.'

'Didn't you press her?'

'It would have looked peculiar,' said Ramble. He was still, Bognor realized, extremely nervous. His colour was very poor and he was shaking.

'I must hurry," said Bognor, 'or I'll lose her. Did she say if she was going to the airport?'

'No. Nothing. You'd better go.' Ramble stood to one side, and Bognor depressed the clutch. 'Don't let anything happen to Prettyboy,' shouted the breeder above the noise of the engine. Bognor smiled, waved and gave a V for victory sign. He didn't feel at all happy now but there was no point in showing it.

He turned left out of the gate and sped down the lane. It was three miles to Tuck Baldring and that was the best way back to civilization. However after only half a mile there was a T-junction and when he reached it there was no sign of the van. Bognor took a calculated risk and headed towards the village. After another mile he came round a bend and almost went into the back of 'Animal Transport's' machine. He braked and slowed, hoping that Coriander wouldn't recognize his car. She had a close enough view of it the other day when Monica had given chase but it was getting dark now and the colours were barely discernible. He put on dipped headlights and fell back.

Coriander was in no hurry, it seemed. She drove steadily and without haste in the direction of London and Bognor had no difficulty in following her. Even when they reached the motorway she stuck to the inside lane at fifty miles an hour and Bognor allowed an articulated heavy lorry to interpose itself between the two vehicles. He could still see her but he was less obtrusive. At the junction with the North Circular Road he gave a little smile of satisfaction as she followed the looping road to the right. That way lay the west of London and a little beyond it, the airport at Heathrow. He hoped that Parkinson had alerted the police. At Hanger Lane she passed across the main Oxford road and continued south still circling the city, and a couple of miles further on, just north of Kew Bridge, she climbed up on to the M4 which, at that point, flies over the suburbs on its way towards Bristol and South Wales. Bognor's satisfaction was becoming almost total. She *had* to be going to the airport and, to judge from the unflustered, almost smug way she was driving, she had no idea she was being followed. As the road hit ground level again he began to relax.

The relaxation was shortlived. A mile or so further on she suddenly turned off the motorway. Bognor almost missed her manoeuvre, but caught himself in time. All his senses came alive once more. Why was she leaving the road? An assignation? A change of plan? She must have spotted him after all. Then, relieved, he saw that this wasn't an exit road but the entrance to the Heston service station. A sign over the main building said, 'Welcome to Granada' and Bognor realized that Miss Cordingley had stopped for a coffee or a pee. It briefly crossed his mind that she could surely have waited until the airport which was not more than ten minutes away, but the thought did not seriously disturb him.

He slowed to little more than walking pace as the van ahead berthed in a parking bay. It was essential that she shouldn't see him but as it was now quite dark there was little chance of it. The car park was full of holiday families heading coastwards and taking a final opportunity to stock up with ice creams and packets of crisps and sweets before the long night drive. There was a constant traffic of humanity and machinery, and parking some fifty yards away Bognor rated his chances of remaining unseen as being exceptionally high. He switched off the lights and sat watching.

The trouble with remaining virtually invisible, himself, was that his powers of observation were correspondingly limited. He could see the van and when the door opened he could see that a lithe figure wearing a cap and flared trousers had got out. However the park was insufficiently lit for him to be able to recognize Coriander. Moreover he couldn't follow her into the restaurant area because under the harsh glare of the overhead strip lighting she would be virtually certain to notice him. However it didn't seem to matter as Coriander's slim silhouette, shoulder bag swaying slightly as she walked, crossed the car park and entered through the swing doors. He took a cheroot from the packet and lit it; got out of the car, stretched, and blew smoke into the darkness; the end of the cigar glowed reassuringly. Everything was going according to plan.

Five minutes later he was sitting, eyes idly scanning the park, when he was aware that the slim silhouette was returning to the van. With an almost studied nonchalance, the shoulder bag was unstrapped, and thrown on to the rear seat. The driver followed it. Seconds later the lights came on and Animal Transport Ltd headed out of the park and back on to the westbound carriageway.

Bognor's first real surprise came a few miles further on. So certain was he that Perfect Prettyboy was about to take off from Heathrow that he himself was indicating to go left at the airport turning. Only when he was travelling down the gentle left-hand bend did he notice, with a start, that the van was continuing straight ahead towards Slough. He frowned. That was very peculiar. He hoped the Heathrow police had not been over-alerted.

At the Slough central turning the van turned off, by-passed Windsor and headed for Bagshot. Bognor knew this route. It was the link between the M4 and M3 motorways. If, as now seemed probable, they were aiming for the M3, then they could end up anywhere from Southampton to Weymouth. That must be it, he thought with a worried frown. The wretched animal was being smuggled out by sea. Probably in the hold of some banana boat. But why? It was so much slower. And no less risky. He tried to stop speculating. It was useless, and while he kept the van fixed firmly in his sights he was in no trouble. The drill would remain the same. He wondered, despite himself, if it would be Weymouth. The only boats leaving there were Channel Island ferries. Unless they were using the Royal Naval base. Hardly likely.

At Micheldever they stuck to the A30, heading for Salisbury. Bognor remembered with a twinge of worried anticipation that this was the way to the Duchess of Dorset's. He prayed that he would be spared another visit to that ill-fated place. Salisbury in turn was by-passed around midnight and then Blandford, silently asleep, was traversed. Three miles outside, the van turned left towards Bere Regis. In Bere it crossed the main road and headed due south, away, thankfully, from Dora Dorset's, which still remained uncomfortably close. Bognor guessed the sea would not be far now—under ten miles. They passed the Royal Armoured Corps at Bovington Camp, crossed the level crossing near Wool Station, illuminated but apparently uninhabited, then immediately afterwards swung left at a sign to Lulworth Cove. Bognor frowned again. As far as he knew Lulworth was little more than a pretty picture on a postcard: all lobster pots and ancient fisherfolk. There would certainly be no cargo ships or passenger steamers, let alone aircraft. On the other

hand it was a smuggler's cove straight from the pages
of romantic fiction. Perhaps a powerful launch or even
a fishing smack to France and then a quick spin to the
nearest French airport, where no quarantine restrictions
operated and, hey presto, New York, Los Angeles,
Bogota or . . . He was musing on this when the van
pulled over to the side of the road and stopped. It was
half past one. Bognor braked hurriedly. They were still
in the village and he reversed quickly behind another
parked car and switched off his lights. He prayed that
Coriander hadn't noticed.

For five minutes he sat and waited, but nothing happened. Another five. Still nothing. He had a small
pencil torch in the glove compartment, and he picked
it out and examined his Automobile Association Guide
with it. As far as he could see this road led only to
Lulworth, though there were turnings which could lead
to Wareham or Weymouth. Neither seemed likely. There
had been more direct routes to both. It occurred to
him suddenly that perhaps Coriander was merely taking a quick nap before embarking. Since he had an
almost certain idea of her destination, now could be the
time to ring Parkinson. He looked around and saw to
his satisfaction that there was a phone booth, not thirty
yards from the car. He tiptoed stealthily towards it and
inside dialled Parkinson's special line, the one which
would automatically be transferred to wherever he was.

'Yes.' The phone had rung several times and the
voice sounded bleary. Parkinson had clearly been
asleep. Bognor, suddenly feeling his own fatigue, en-
vied him.

'It's me,' he said, *sotto voce,* 'I'm in Wool.'

'Where?'

'Wool. North of Lulworth. About four miles north,
I think. I can see the van with the dog in it. They're
parked. I think possibly they're resting before making
their break. My guess is that they'll run for it at dawn.'

'Don't be so bloody melodramatic,' said Parkinson.
'Why dawn? You're always guessing and you're invariably wrong.'

'But will you alert the police?' asked Bognor. 'The van has "Animal Transport Ltd" written on the side and it has to be heading for Lulworth. From what I can see you can cut it off by setting up road blocks on the Lulworth to Wareham and the Lulworth to Weymouth roads. They'd better have a boat of some kind to cut off the sea and I'll be behind her.'

'Big deal,' said Parkinson laconically, 'I'll talk to the local constabulary and tell them what you're doing. Remember to keep in touch.'

Bognor replaced the receiver very gently and retraced his footsteps slowly and tentatively; back in the car he lit a cigar and settled down to wait.

He had trouble keeping awake and was dozing fitfully when he heard the sound of an engine starting. He looked at his watch and saw that it was just after five. He hadn't been so wrong about dawn. The morning had got to the stage where shapes were visible but only in two dimensional form, and where colours were muted to a stage only just more gaudy than black, white and grey. Birds were being noisy but otherwise the country had barely woken. Not even an early morning tractor disturbed the peace. The van swung back on to the road and set off toward Lulworth. Bognor waited until it had turned the corner and followed in slow pursuit. He kept his lights off to avoid arousing suspicion, and hoped that the police were in position. It would be absurd to have got so far and then to lose.

At the bottom of the long hill to the cove the road narrowed and there was a large public car park. Bognor parked well away from it and got out to walk. The van had stopped in the park and he watched in the shadow of a cottage as the driver came round to the back, opened the doors and took out a crate with a handle. He could scarcely resist a smile of triumph. Dog and smuggler heading for the water's edge. Perfect. From behind he heard a car which stopped abruptly. Footsteps followed the slamming of its door and in a moment an unmistakably policeman's voice enquired, 'Mr Bognor of the Board of Trade?'

He turned to see a heavy figure in blue, wearing a hat adorned with scrambled egg. The man carried gloves and a cane, which meant a gratifying degree of seniority.

'Yes,' he said, 'Simon Bognor.' They shook hands. 'That,' he pointed to the disappearing smuggler as she walked down the narrow street, 'is your woman, and the poodle's in the basket thing she's carrying.'

'Fine,' said the policeman. 'We have a launch standing by outside the cove. I suggest we follow at our leisure. I'll just make sure they're alerted.' He walked back to the car and Bognor heard the crackle of electricity from the wireless set as instructions were given. Then, together, they sauntered downhill.

When they arrived at the seashore the drama was just beginning to unfold. As they rounded the last cottage and came alongside the cafeteria and the chandler's shop they could see that a seagoing cabin cruiser ornamented with wires and radar was just beginning to power towards the narrow entrance to the cove. Standing in the stern was the wasp waisted figure in the costermonger cap.

'Shall we row after them?' asked the policeman, waving in the direction of a dinghy on the pebbles a few yards away. Bognor nodded and together they heaved the little boat into the water, took an oar each and paddled across the famous horseshoe harbour. The motor boat was a hundred yards ahead of them and not at full throttle. Half-way across the water, the two rowers rested and turned their craft round, the better to observe operations. Just as the smuggler's vessel approached the open sea, just as its engines were revved up preparatory to an exultant charge towards France, a smart blue launch came into view, almost blocking the exit. The smugglers threw their engines into reverse and Bognor could hear a voice through a megaphone dimly. 'Heave to,' it said, 'we are coming aboard.' He rested his chin on his oars as the police boat went alongside the cruiser and two uniformed men sprang on board. A moment later they jumped back on board their boat, accompanied this time by a captive figure and the crate containing Perfect Prettyboy.

'Very neat indeed,' said Bognor, appreciatively. 'Let's meet them on *terra firma,* shall we?' Saying which he dipped his oar into the sea and together they rowed sedately if clumsily back to the land. They arrived there at almost exactly the same moment as the police launch, and as they struck the beach Bognor heard a greeting which made his stomach lurch in a sudden ghastly anticipation of despair.

9

'Morning, Mr Bognor. You're up very early, and you seem to have brought a great many friends.' Looking up to the deck of the police boat Bognor saw that the sylph-like figure in the immaculate suiting was not, as it had been the previous night, Coriander Cordingley. It had been transformed into Cecil Handyside. The dog transporter touched his faintly absurd corduroy cap in a gesture of courteous greeting. 'I was just goin' fishin' when I was waylaid by your colleagues here. I wonder if you'd be so kind as to ask them to remove themselves.'

Bognor was not so easily discouraged.

'The dog,' he shouted back through cupped hands. 'The dog. You're forgetting the dog.'

Handyside put a hand to his ear affecting not to hear and then jumped down on to the beach, followed by two policemen.

'I thought,' said Bognor's companion, 'that we were pursuing a lady.' His tones were frosty with suspended belief.

'We were,' said Bognor. His mind, more than usually slowed by his long drive and sleepless night, struggled to cope with the sex change. It could only have been at the service station. Coriander must have left the car in the gloom, met Handyside in the restaurant, exchanged car keys. Then the figure who had come back to the van must have been Handyside. Bognor tried to cast his mind back to the scene and recalled the slim

silhouette with the shoulder bag. It was conceivable. . . .
He hadn't managed to recognize the face or even the
clothes, only the outline and the walk. Handyside and
Coriander had, it dawned on him, tolerably similar
figures, and a sexy wiggling walk was easily simulated.
It was a risky swop, but it had worked.

'Sorry, I didn't quite catch . . .' It was Handyside,
standing before him, unmistakable now and preening
himself.

'The dog,' said Bognor, 'Ramble's champion poodle.
It's in your crate, up there on the deck. I know. And
don't think you'll get away with it. That dog is now
positively and demonstrably identifiable.'

'Could well be,' drawled Handyside, lizard-like. 'Only
it just doesn't happen to be here.'

'Don't give me that,' said Bognor. 'I want to see inside that crate. Now. Will you open it yourself or am
I going to have to force it?'

There was a moment of tense silence before Handyside answered. A pair of gulls wheeled and mewed at
each other in a desultory dog-fight, the small waves
lapped gently on the pebbles and the police, grown
dangerously neutral, looked on curiously. Then the
smuggler shrugged.

'Don't know what you're ramblin' about,' he said,
'but you're welcome to look. Not that there's any law
against fishin' gear. Not to my knowledge.'

He turned round and headed back to the police
launch. Bognor followed him and scrambled aboard.
The police gathered round, curious but not, Bognor
realized sadly, very friendly. He was afraid they thought
him mistaken, and worse, incompetent.

Handyside paused theatrically, then with a flourish,
lifted the lid of the crate, which was made from canvas. There was, as he had said, no dog. Instead there
was a quantity of telescoped aluminium tubing, some
twine and some vicious hooks. Even to the uninitiated,
like Bognor, it looked like fishing tackle.

Silence descended once more, broken finally by Bognor.

'I'm sorry,' he said, 'but shortly after eight o'clock last night a miniature poodle, Perfect Prettyboy, was loaded on to your van at the kennels of Mr Albert Ramble. That dog must be here. We shall just have to search until we find it.'

Even as he said the words he knew that he was wrong. Perfect Prettyboy was even now on its way . . . he consulted his watch . . . worse, had probably arrived in New York. He had failed.

'I wonder,' he turned back to the senior policeman, 'I wonder if you could possibly go through the van. That dog must be somewhere. It is . . .' he concluded feebly, 'very small.'

He knew it was hopeless, but he had to do something. Even as the police grudgingly acquiesced his mind ran swiftly over the possibilities. There were only two. He could either confess to Parkinson. That would be humiliating and unproductive. This time Parkinson really would in his characteristically picturesque phrase, 'have his guts for garters.' He would be fired with ignominy and without pay. His pride and his purse would not allow it. The alternative was to continue his pursuit of Perfect Prettyboy. Parkinson would never consent to such a course of action. Too expensive. Too speculative. Too, he had to face it, too Bognorish. He sighed, and felt in his inside jacket pocket. His wallet, bulging with credit cards, and his passport were both there. Together they would get him to the States before anyone realized. He would telephone Watherspoon for the precise address of Edgar J. Eagerly's Dog Centre and go there with all due haste. It was a shade risky, but he knew intuitively that he would find both Coriander and the poodle there. The alternative was too grim.

'Excuse me,' he said to the policeman at his elbow, 'I must make a phone call.' So saying, he set off back up the road towards the Mini in the car park. There was no time to lose and he could not afford to suggest his course of action to the police. They would have no alternative but to let Handyside go, and no doubt they would make formal complaint to Parkinson. At the moment, that was the least of his worries.

He was airborne before lunch and the achievement gave him a compensating satisfaction after earlier disasters. The return journey to Heathrow took little more than three hours. He had found a flight with plenty of empty seats and paid for it on his Diner's Card. Wather-spoon had given him the address of the Dog Centre with the added information that it was no more than three and a half hours' fast driving on the Thru-Way from Kennedy Airport. He had also contacted Monica and told her where he was going. She had been resigned though greatly alarmed. He had even persuaded her to telephone Parkinson and tell him that he, Bognor, was coming personally to explain the débâcle. That gave him breathing space. By the time Parkinson realized that he was AWOL, he would have reached the Dog Centre. He settled back in his seat and absentmindedly ate the olive from his dry martini. This morning had been appalling but things would scarcely deteriorate further. If he could run the little poodle and Miss Cordingley to earth at the home of Edgar J. Eagerly, he would have come back from an apparently impossible situation. He thought he could.

At Kennedy it was baking hot and he hired a car, using his American Express Card this time—a manoeu-vre which made him feel that he'd spent less money than if he'd used the Diner's Card a second time. The car—a Chevrolet—seemed monstrously cumbersome by his standards but had automatic gears, a luxury which diminished the horrors of driving on American roads.

After an uneasy half hour during which he repeated-ly turned the windscreen wipers on when trying to in-dicate a change of direction, he acclimatized himself to the car, and even settled into a sort of routine. The road was boring as only six-lane highways can be and although he was driving north-east towards Lake On-tario he might as well have been on the M1 south of

Birmingham or the Autobahn near Stuttgart. It was just concrete and high speed tin. After an hour and a half he stopped for a hamburger and a strawberry milk shake, then continued. His destination lay, according to Watherspoon, between two small towns called Old Forge and Big Moose in a mountain area named the Adirondacks. Bognor, who had only twice before been to America, both times years earlier, had dimly heard of the Adirondacks. Or thought he had. He might, he conceded, have been muddling them with the Alleghenies or the Appalachians.

A sign told him that he was not far short of Schenectady. From there he continued until Utica then struck north for the mountains. If he got as far as Rome he'd gone wrong. He smiled to himself. The Americans certainly had curious names. He'd noticed Copenhagen on the map too. The sight stirred unhappy memories of Raffles, the Chewing Gum Dog, and he frowned. He hoped this would be a more successful mission. He rubbed his chin thoughtfully with his left hand and realized with sudden horror that it was prickly with beard. He hadn't shaved for an age. Nor had he brought any shaving kit with him. Nor any luggage. He frowned. His sleep had been fitful to say the least. A few snatched moments in the Mini near Lulworth. A few more in the plane. He was, to coin a phrase, dog tired, and he'd need to be on his mettle in a few hours' time.

The Utica exit was clearly signed and, rather to his surprise, he located the road towards the Adirondacks with no problem. It was evidently a holiday centre for the side of the road was littered with invitations to sample the fishing and swimming, the bed and the board at various places in the Adirondacks National Park. The road itself was peopled with holidaymakers heading in the same direction. They seemed brasher and more self-assured than those he'd seen only yesterday near Heathrow airport. They drove more assertively and they managed to keep all their luggage inside the car, instead of on the roof.

Gradually the scenery assumed an almost Scottish air. He passed a small lake with jagged rocky shores, dotted with rowing boats and fishermen sitting in them, lines floating out behind. Fir trees began to predominate and he was reminded uneasily of a disastrous visit to Mc-Crum Castle, during an earlier and equally ill-starred investigation.

He was musing inconsequentially and becoming progressively drowsier when, out of the corner of his eye, he noticed a sign to Whispering Moose Gorge. This, he recalled, was the postal address of the Dog Centre. He reversed and turned off down the road which now passed through thick conifers and rose steadily. After ten minutes he emerged from the forest and saw that the road continued along the ridge of the hill, while below and to the left a tarmacadam drive wound down hill to another lake. On its shore there was a cluster of ranch style buildings and between him and them there was a fence, surrounded by barbed wire, which from his position some half a mile away, seemed to be about seven feet high. No sign indicated the place's identity but Bognor caught, on the thin breeze which drifted towards him, the plaintive and distinctive melody of hounds, baying, he decided, with a slight smile, for broken biscuit.

He drove slowly towards the noise. At the wire barrier there was a gate, also seven feet high, and along the top of it ran more barbed wire as well as another strand which looked to him as if it was electric. The only sign said 'Keep Out. Strictly Private. Dangerous Dogs'. By the side of the gate there was a speaking grille, and above it a pivoting box with a lens. At first Bognor wondered if it was radar, then realized with a start that it was more likely to be a closed circuit TV camera. Undeterred by the warnings he left the Chevrolet and advanced on the tube. He was still a yard short of it when it spoke.

'Name?' it said, demanding it in a nasal North American accent.

'Bognor.'

'Rank? Title? Or other distinguishing feature?' Bognor had the uneasy feeling that he was dealing with a computerized tape. It was a far cry from the Duchess of Dorset's kennels, or Ailsa Potts'.

'Board of Trade, London, Special Investigator.'

He said it with a brusque self-confidence he was far from feeling. The dogs sounded alarmingly savage. They were still barking.

'Purpose of visit?'

He looked down at his suedes. It was a good question. He suddenly felt very vulnerable and slightly absurd. It was a long way to have come on what was, if he was honest, no more than an off-chance.

'To see Mr Eagerly.'

'Identification.'

He produced his card and held it up to what he assumed was the camera. There was a whirring noise. 'Please wait,' said the machine, and he felt as he always did after feeding his banker's card into the machine which dispensed banknotes. Guilty anticipation. The fear that the machine would recognize him for the bankrupt he really was. He stood, waiting. Even the vast, chrome-covered Chevrolet was alien and there was nothing in the stark highland scenery, let alone the security fencing, to make him feel at home. Only the clothes he stood in were comfortably and unmistakably British and his own.

'Please enter.' The machine jolted him out of his reverie with another metallic command, and as it spoke the heavy gates creaked back along ill-greased runners. He swallowed hard. This was his last chance to turn tail and run. The dogs sang greedily and the gates crunched to a halt. For a moment he hesitated, then got back in the car and drove slowly forward towards the residence of Edgar J. Eagerly. As he did he saw in the driving mirror that the great gates had shut behind him.

The buildings were another half-mile further on across the Adirondacks equivalent of parkland—a field of tough, tufted grass dotted with rabbit warrens. Then he came to a group of low timbered sheds with runs outside some of them. He knew enough now to realize that these were kennels. Past them on the very side of the lake was the house. It too was timber and constructed in a style which Bognor mentally categorized as 'millionaire frontiersman'. At first glance it could have been a log cabin. On second it was unmistakably Beverly Hills.

As he approached it, the front door opened. But no one emerged. Instead another disembodied, metallic voice bade him enter. Still more gingerly he did and was further disconcerted when that door, too, shut softly behind him.

The hall, in which he now stood, was heavily carpeted, walled in thick chocolate velvet and dominated by an enormous, garish portrait of a man with three ferocious looking dogs of a breed Bognor could not recognize. The style in which the picture was painted was, however, quite unmistakable, and he had no need to glance at the initials 'C.C.' in the bottom right-hand corner to confirm his impression. He lit a cheroot and was just exhaling smoke in the direction of the picture when he was greeted from behind.

'Mr Bognor.' The word was pronounced 'Bahgnur' with practically all the emphasis on the first syllable. He spun as speedily as the thick pile of the carpet would allow and came face to face with the subject of Miss Cordingley's portrait. His complexion was not so high nor his features so well proportioned as in the lurid painting, but otherwise the one was a passable likeness of the other. Edgar J. Eagerly had iron grey hair and tinted glasses, a lumberjack's checked shirt, jodhpurs, riding boots, and a ridiculous tuft of goatee at the end of his chin.

'Mr Eagerly,' said Simon.

'Bourbon, Mr Bahgnur?' said Mr Eagerly. 'I hope you like my portrait. One of Coriander's finest works.' He came and stood alongside Bognor and stared briefly at the picture through the glasses, which were a pale burgundy, like Swiss wine.

'Bourbon, Mr Bognor,' he repeated, this time as a statement instead of an invitation. As he walked towards the double doors, they parted before him admitting both men to a gallery-like room overlooking the lake. Like the hall it was opulent and heavily ornamented, this time with canine pictures by rather better known artists. Gainsborough's *White Dogs* hung above the mantelpiece and along the wall by the bronze of a St Bernard there were papillons by Rubens, Watteau, Fragonard and Boucher. Opposite were Constable's *The Haywain* and *The Cornfield,* one including a collie and the other a farm dog. Bognor studied them while Eagerly poured a generous slug of bourbon from a decanter shaped like a dachshund. The glass in which it was served had a poodle on its side. Bognor held it up to the light, then sipped it. It was very warming, and he realized, unexpectedly, much needed.

'These reproductions,' he said, waving his arm about the room in the direction of the pictures, 'they're very good.'

'Reproductions?' asked Mr Eagerly. 'I'm sorry, Mr Bognor, what reproductions? We have no reproductions here.'

'*The Haywain,*' said Bognor, 'is in the National Gallery in London.' He didn't know much about art, but that much he did know.

Mr Eagerly pushed his spectacles to the end of his nose and stared over the top of them appraisingly. 'No reproductions here, Mr Bognor, authenticity and absolute originality are the passport to perfection. My father taught me so. Coriander, incidentally, apologizes for keeping you waiting. We hadn't expected you so soon.' Bognor flinched. 'But perhaps you'd like to see the poodle,' continued his host. 'No doubt you'll be happy to see that Perfect Prettyboy is in perfect health, though I'm bound to admit that a lady's satchel is not the ideal contrivance for transatlantic transportation.'

Bognor took a deep draught of bourbon.

'Am I to understand,' he began, in the Board of Trade style which he kept for special occasions like this, 'that you admit to having the poodle Perfect Prettyboy on your premises unlawfully and that you admit to being party to its illegal smuggling from Great Britain by Miss Cordingley?'

'Of course, Simon dear.' Once more he spun half successfully on his heel, this time to see Coriander Cordingley, hair piled in a golden beehive on her head, crimson lips parted in an expression of happy triumph, her entire body visible under the lightly transparent white robe which was all she wore.

'Hello,' he said fatuously. 'What is all this?'

She laughed musically, though to Bognor the music had a threateningly discordant sound, like the Dead March played on a penny whistle.

'All this,' she said, 'means that the game is up, doesn't it? She lisped, 'Or "don't it?" as Cecil would say. You've tracked me down. Caught us poodle-handed. I'm not going to bother with fetching poor little Prettyboy because he's had a dreadfully tiring day, but his tattoo's still there all right, so he won't come to any harm.'

'Good,' said Bognor, at sea and wondering if the glimmer of hope he could faintly distinguish was a lighthouse or wreckers on the rocks. 'In that case I'd better use your telephone.'

He turned to Eagerly dredging as much menace as he could muster from the dregs of his fatigue.

'Your friend is certainly a trier,' said Eagerly talking over his head to Coriander, 'real bulldog spirit. I think he deserves another bourbon.' He took Bognor's drink and poured more whisky into it.

'Let's go outside,' said Coriander, 'and explain. It's a beautiful evening.' They walked out through more electric doors and sat on a verandah on cane furniture. The sun was setting over the lake, just fading behind a mountain top on the far bank. 'Spruce Lake Mountain,' said Eagerly. 'Fine sight.'

'Now,' said Coriander kicking off her shoes and putting her naked painted feet on the table. 'You, Simon dear, are here because we want you to be here. We

decided a long time ago that your attentions were becoming tedious. We didn't think, frankly, that you'd be
bright enough to follow Raffles to Denmark—particularly in view of my immaculate artwork—and after
that we decided you'd have to be removed. So we arranged with Albert Ramble . . .'

'*With* Albert Ramble?'

She laughed at him. 'Everyone has his price,' she
said, 'though I expect poor Albert is under the illusion
that he's playing a double game. We arranged for his
little poodle to be smuggled out, and we made as sure
as we could that you would make a complete fool of
yourself, as publicly as possible. Which I hear from
Cecil Handyside you did quite beautifully.' She tittered
and crossed her legs. Despite the unpleasantness of his
situation Bognor felt himself aroused as he had before.
'Once that had happened, we argued that you would
be quite unable to face your superiors and would have
to resort to what for want of a better word we'll call
your initiative. We gave you enough clues. I even reminded you about darling old Edgar J. the other evening at the Savoy. Remember?'

Bognor remembered all too well.

'You see,' she stretched lazily, 'you see we decided
that this was much the easiest place to stage an unfortunate accident. Besides it ties in with Edgar's guard
dog research. We'll just say that you must have managed to get through the barrier and that naturally the
dogs then . . . er, disposed of you.'

'What about the car?'

'That's no problem. It's quite easy to put it back
outside the gate. Alternatively we could say that you
were received and entertained and then, contrary to
all warnings, went snooping about in the dead of night,
only to be attacked by the animals . . . after all, you
are known to make a habit of nocturnal prowling,
aren't you?'

She sucked her teeth and made little tutting noises.

Eagerly spoke for the first time for ages. 'The dogs
are remarkable, Mr Bognor. You'll be making a unique

contribution to canine genetic development and the study of aggression in the canine when deprived of normal food. The dog requires forty-three different nutrients, Mr Bognor, but for the past few days prior to your arrival I have to say that the two animals we have in mind for this experiment have been deprived of any nutrient whatever. Water is all they have had.' He chuckled softly.

'Edgar,' said Coriander, changing the subject, 'be a pet and fetch me a Tom Collins.' He rose obediently and went inside. It was getting dark now and mosquitoes from the lake were rising towards them.

'Do you swim?' asked Coriander.

'More or less.'

'Oh goody,' she said, 'in that case we'll start you off from the island. Much more fun. Now what do you want to know before we begin? Since you're not going to be able to pass anything on I'll tell you absolutely everything you want to know.'

Bognor winced. 'Don't be so sure,' he said, 'I've got out of some pretty difficult situations in the past.' He thought of the Marquess of Lydeard's bison, Viscount Wimbledon's savage attack near Sloane Square, the similar assault at Beaubridge Friary. None, he conceded, had been quite as impossible seeming as this.

'So sweet and optimistic,' said Coriander.

Eagerly came back with the Tom Collins and she told him the whole story which, maddeningly, was almost precisely as he had already conjectured. The prize movers in the scheme were herself and Handyside. She made the contacts and provided most of the brains, Handyside the mechanical know-how. Eagerly was their American executive. Dora Dorset supplied some animals. So had many others. They had tried to co-opt Ailsa Potts but she had been obstinate. Hence the demise of Whately Wonderful, poisoned with strychnine by Handyside.

'And poor Rose?' asked Bognor, aghast.

'Cecil's work,' she said, sipping decorously at her long drink. 'The murder didn't upset him, though I'm

afraid the sexual aspect of it was rather a trial. I persuaded him that it was essential.'

'Pocklington?'

'Percy,' said Coriander, 'can be tiresome, but clients
have to be guaranteed some success in the shows they
enter. Percy is a useful insurance policy.'

'And the dogs are smuggled in how?'

'Only very tiny dogs go in handbags after a dose of
knockout drops. Bigger dogs are more complicated.
We do sometimes use boats. Lulworth, too, so you
weren't far wrong. Anything else?'

'Yes. In Copenhagen. There was a message. Something about wafers and honey.'

'A gentle tease. A play on my name. It's Exodus
16.31. Manna from heaven is like coriander which is
in turn like wafers made with honey. Remember?'

Bognor didn't remember. The sun had gone now
and he could hardly see the other two. 'Is there much
money in it? Is it worth the risk?'

'There's enough. Partly I do it for fun, but I've always said I aim to make a lot of money so Edgar and
I have a lucrative additional game. Drugs. You make
the animals swallow encapsulated narcotics, then when
we get in here we wait till it produces its stools as the
dog world so elegantly describes dog crap. Edgar has
a special machine for analysing it and we eliminate the
drugs and pass on. Quite neat.'

Bognor was silent. Eventually he said, 'That just
about wraps it up. No more questions.'

'But surely, Mr Bognor,' said Eagerly's voice out of
the darkness, 'you want to know what we have in store
for you?'

'I'm sure it's unpleasant,' he said, 'and horribly ef-
fective from what you've suggested so far.'

'I won't bore you with the details,' said Eagerly,
'unless you'd care to dine first. I had intended to set
you off before dinner but it could wait until afterwards.
We have some very delicious trout from the lake here.'

'Thank you, no.' Bognor would normally have enjoyed trout, but he had always found the idea of the condemned man's breakfast peculiarly repulsive.

'It's simple then,' said Eagerly. 'For years now I have been attempting to breed the perfect guard dog. A touch of Dobermann here, a pinch of Alsatian, a dash of Rottweiler—a more than generous helping of Tibetan mastiff, so fierce a dog that Aristotle thought it half tiger—and a suspicion of our own Chesapeake Bay. They have webbed feet, as you may know, and our security companies are increasingly interested in a dog that can perform usefully in water. I think I now have a prototype which is ready for revealing to the world, but I have yet to conduct as telling an experiment as this. I propose to give them a portion of your clothing to familiarize them with your scent. Then you may have a ten-minute start to swim across the lake from the island. Normally this exercise would destroy your trail, but I think my breeding has given these animals a highly enough developed nose to get over that. In any case they have all the time in the world to find you, though the sooner they do the happier we shall all be.' Bognor sensed the malevolent smile though he could not see it. He shivered. The man was worse than Handyside.

'What if I escape from the . . . compound?' he asked.

His captors laughed in unison. 'Surely you saw,' said Coriander. 'It's like a stockade. No one could get out of that. Not even an Olympic pole vaulter and, Simon dear, you're scarcely that.'

Eagerly spoke again. 'It shouldn't take long unless you resist, in which case I suppose it could be painful. They've been trained to go for the throat. One bite and you're gone.' He chuckled again. 'Forget the boundary fence, Mr Bognor,' he said. 'If you get as far as that the dogs are a disaster, and believe you me, they are *not* a disaster.'

'If that's all,' said Coriander, 'I think we ought to be off. I'm rather peckish.'

'What if I make a break for it now?' asked Bognor, knowing the answer would be gloomy.

'You'd get about a hundred yards if you were fast off the mark,' she said. 'Edgar has staff even if you haven't noticed them.'

He tried to collect his thoughts as they walked down to the landing stage. Alongside there was an open dory with a searchlight in the bows which Eagerly turned on. Within seconds they were chugging slowly across towards the island. He sighed. It was only a few hours ago that he had been rowing across the water on the other side of the Atlantic. Then he had been on the point of a great triumph. Now he was on the point of death. It was a dramatic and depressing transformation, and he could think of nothing except the reactions of his friends and colleagues. He wondered how many would be sad at his going.

There was another jetty on the far side and they moved there. It was about a hundred yards away. The three of them stepped ashore, Coriander and Eagerly almost jaunty, Bognor limp and tired. Ahead was a square wooden hut, and Eagerly pointed his heavy torch towards it. 'They're in there,' he said unnecessarily, for a blood-curdling howling and yelping now came from the building.

'They've heard us,' said Coriander. 'Edgar calls them Haldeman and Ehrlichman. He's a Democrat.'

Inside the building the two animals were in separate compartments. They were heavy, well-muscled beasts with massive heads, yellow eyes, stumpy tails and, as Eagerly had said, webbed feet. Already their muzzles were flecked with white foam and they snarled at all three of them from the other side of their iron bars.

Bognor wiped his forehead with the back of his hand and was only vaguely surprised to find that although the night was now cool, his hand came away covered in sweat.

'Since you're swimming,' said Coriander, 'I'd take all your clothes off. We can give them to the dogs for scent.'

'All?' snapped Bognor, his voice rising several octaves. 'All?'

'Don't be so British,' said Coriander, starting to undo his tie. 'You can keep your underpants on.'

He did as he was told, pushing her away as he undressed. He felt desperately ill, as if he was going to be sick. Perhaps, he thought, if he just threw a fit and lay gibbering at their feet they might relent. But no. He could see from their expression that they were enjoying it too much. Bloody sadists. He retched noisily as he pulled off his socks, then stood flabby and forlorn in his aertex Y-front pants.

'Goodbye, Simon,' said Coriander. 'You have about fifteen minutes. Make the most of them.'

Eagerly was throwing his tweed suit to Haldeman and Ehrlichman as he left the hut and ran to the lake. He was shivering as if he had malaria, and still felt sick, but as he hit the reedy water his head cleared and he seemed to wake. Breast stroke was all he could do, but in his panic and terror he swam fast and reached the bank without mishap. He struggled out and sprinted off, panting heavily now, partly from fear but more because he was chronically unfit. Behind him he could still hear the frustrated sound of the dogs. They could not have been released yet. He had no idea what he was doing, so he ran, his bare flat feet finding the springy grass quite comfortable. Somewhere at the back of his mind was the thought that if he could only reach the boundary barrier some miracle might occur, but the miracle came early.

Just as the baying of the dogs changed key, to an undoubted noise of pursuit in which he could distinguish human cries of encouragement, his foot twisted on something soggy and furry, and he stumbled, then sprawled full length. He reached out to see what it was and picked up a small, dead animal. It smelt putrid. Behind him he could hear splashing and fevered whining. The barks were approaching. He looked down at the small animal and wondered absurdly what it would be. A rabbit? A marmot? Hell, it didn't matter. It was meat. He clutched it in one hand and staggered on, breath failing. Behind he heard the barking change pitch again. They must have emerged from the water. Not long now. He held fast to his salvation. What had they said? They went for the throat. He groaned and tried to coax more speed from his aching muscles. The dogs were gaining rapidly. He could hear the thundering of their feet, and the panting of their breath, then as he sensed the warmth of their bodies immediately behind him he let out a great shriek with all that remained of his breath, hurled the dead rodent wildly behind him and sprinted. There was a sudden cry from the pursuers which degenerated into a scuffling snarling and growling and the unmistakable sound of bone being broken. He stole a glance behind him and saw to his intense relief that his stratagem had worked. Haldeman and Ehrlichman each had one end of their trophy in their jaws and they were, he sensed, about to fight bitterly for it. He turned back and charged on. Suddenly without warning he cannoned into the barrier. It almost knocked him unconscious and he lay there for a second listening to the dreadful growling behind him. Then he stood and reached up. If he stretched he could just reach the top of the fence. Above it, he knew, was wire, but . . .

After several jumps he secured a handhold. After a period of rest he managed to clamber up until he could touch the wire. He recoiled instantly with a shriek. The electric current was running all right. Behind him the dogs were still fighting. He smiled with grim pleasure as he realized the interpretation that Coriander and Mr Eagerly would be putting on it. No doubt they would be eating their trout and filling their minds with horrid imaginings of his body being torn apart. He shuddered and leapt back at the fence. He could dangle from it, but he could get no higher. If he raised his legs he might just evade the clutches of a leaping dog. But not for long. He returned to the ground to wait for the dogs to catch him. It could not be long now. So near and yet so far. Oh God. He started to gibber unintel-ﾗbly. The lake water was making him cold; he was ﾗﾗﾗ;ed; he was terrified. And, as he listened, he

thought he could hear the dogs coming towards him.
He leapt back at the fence and as he did, heard a second miracle. It was the spook-like sound of a siren and
it was approaching at speed. He dangled. Beneath him
he heard the dogs—or was it just one? It sounded
weary and half bored too. He hoisted his legs as high
as he could and prayed. The dog snarled and snif-
fled. The siren got louder, stopped. Away to his right
he heard voices. Quite distinctly the word 'name?' came
drifting across the grass in a thin metallic voice. The
dog snarled again with renewed menace. He took a
risk, sucked as much air as he could into his drained
lungs and shouted again and again 'Help . . . help . . .'
Shortly afterwards he must have passed out. Later he
remembered more voices. Shouting. Shots. A crash.
Another shot. And finally a policeman, unlike any
policeman he'd met before, in a flat peaked cap and
shirtsleeves, and he was looking up at him from behind
a very powerful torch, and he was chewing gum sar-
donically, and all he said as he looked at Bognor hanging dripping from the stockade in his underpants, all
he said as he kicked at the canine corpse with the toe
of one heavy black boot, was, 'Hi, Mac.'

After that he remembered nothing until the moment
when he woke in a neatly laundered hospital bed. As
he focused he hoped he would see a beautiful nurse at
the end of the bed. Or at least Monica. Instead, to his
horror, it was Parkinson.

He recited the stock, clichéd questions about who,
why, what and where and waited as Parkinson explained that he was in an infirmary in Utica, New York
State, and would be returning next day.

He began to apologize and Parkinson cut him short.
'Save it for your girl friend,' he said. 'She told me
where you'd gone. I rang New York and mentioned
Eagerly. They went spare. They've been after him for
years for drugs. They'd also intercepted a highly suspicious telephone call from our friend Handyside. It's
my fault. I'd no idea we were looking for narcotics, I

thought we were simply dealing with some bloody shaggy dog story.'

Simon Bognor closed his eyes and smiled a sad, simple smile. 'I suppose you could say we were sold a pup,' he murmured.